WHOOPS! I WOKE

THE DEAD

by

JOSEPH RUBAS

NIGHTMARE PRESS
Louisville, KY

Nightmare Press is the horror imprint of Frightening
Floyds Publications

Edited by Jacob Floyd
Cover Art by Mason Matlaga
Graphic Design by L.A. Spooner

Thank you for reading! If you like the book, please leave a review on Amazon and Goodreads. Reviews help authors and publishers spread the word.

To keep up with more Nightmare Press news, join the Anubis Press Dynasty on Facebook.

To Diego Martinez,
My friend

Also by Joseph Rubas

After Midnight
Shades

WHOOPS! I WOKE

THE DEAD

by

JOSEPH RUBAS

INTRODUCTION

My name is Alex Warner and, boy, do I have a story to tell *you*. It's full of action, romance, drama, comedy, and stars yours truly - basically, it's the greatest story ever told and I envy you for getting to kick back and enjoy it. I know if *I* was hearing this for the first time, I'd pee with excitement.

Yeah, it's *that* jaw-dropping.

So grab an adult diaper, a bag of chips, and get comfy, because it starts…..now.

First of all, I gotta set the scene a little bit. That's how we writers do; can't neglect *that* detail or your readers will imagine the story taking place in a blank void or something. Like I said, my name is Alex and I'm the coolest person ever. Close your eyes and picture a beautiful, stunning, ethereal, gorgeous, bodacious half-Hispanic girl with silky, waxy, flaxen black hair, dark eyes, and caramel skin.

(By the way, yes, I'm using a thesaurus to help me write this and yes, I *kind* of go overboard sometimes).

Anyway, back to the girl. She's tall, exudes self-confidence, and carries herself with grace and dignity...until she trips over something and falls down, but that doesn't happen very often. She's

1

aloof, mysterious, you see her and you're like, "Man, she looks cool; I wish I was her."

That girl is me. I'm sixteen, fun-loving, and adventurous. I light up the room with my quick wit, acerbic tongue, and...whew, this is harder than I thought. Just take my word for it, I'm awesome. I promise.

I live in Picketts Meade, Virginia with my mom, my dad, and my cousin Jessy. It's a small place where not much happens. You know: Quaint, picturesque, charming, rustic, a real hole-in-the-wall. You got an arcade full of old games, the library, and the park - that's pretty much it for nightlife. Big, comfortable old houses line narrow, shaded streets, storefronts flank Main, and the railroad runs right through the middle of town - honk, honk, comin' through, Jess.

But seriously, train whistles *will* wake you up at night.

My dad (where my terminal whiteness comes from) owns Frank's Diner and my mom (the Latino of the bunch) teaches math at the high school. Yuck, amirite? Of all the subjects she could have picked...she picked math. EYEROLL. Math sucks. I hate math. I'm more of a history and creative writing kind of gal. Yes, I dabble in the literary arts from time to time. Luckily for Stephen King, I don't do it more often; otherwise, his publisher would kick him to the curb and give his contract to me. That's to say, my horror fics *rock*.

Sorry, getting distracted.

Back to my family (*mi familia* in Spanish). My dad's the lamest dude to ever live. On weekends he wears cargo shorts and sandals with socks and

2

he *loves* nineties music. I tease him all the time but I secretly love him to death. He's hardworking, honest, fair, and has a heart of gold...that he hides under constant bragging and complaining. If a big, buff dude comes on TV, Dad's go-to reaction is, 'I can take him.' He grouses like an old man and unironically says, 'Back in my day.'

Calm down, buddy, your day was, like, 1998. Not much has changed since then.

Before he met my mom, he served in the army; he enlisted after 9-11, saw combat in Afghanistan and Iraq, and came home in 2005. And, brother, he will never let you forget it. *It's because of me you don't speak Arabic,* he'll say, and if Mom asks him to take out the trash, he'll beg off because *Gee, hun, I'm an American hero. Make Alex do it.*

Well then.

He doesn't really mean it, though. Like me, he kids around a lot.

My Mom, on the other hand, is a stick-in-the-mud. Just like you'd expect a teacher to be. It's not that she's really strict or humorless or anything, it's...well...

How do I put this? She's constantly on my back about learning Spanish and stuff. *You gotta keep in touch with your heritage, Alex; speak the Mother Tongue, Alex; here, put the burger down and have a taco, Alex.*

Okay, she doesn't really say that last one, but she is *very* adamant that I learn, know, and respect my Mexican ancestry. Look, I get it, that kind of thing is vital and all, but I just don't see the point. My dad's white, my sister's white, I'm basically white, this town's white...

That's to say: I don't feel a connection with Mexican culture. It's not mine. I've never been to Mexico, I don't know anything about it, I was born in America, I live in America, and what right do I have to put on a sombrero and celebrate Sinko Da Myo? It's like...you ever see those people at Oktoberfest or whatever pounding their chests about being German...and the last full-blooded German in their family died fifty generations ago? It strikes me as fake, you know? Like...sit down, white boy, you aren't German. Culture is something that we're born into, shaped by, something that influences us from our earliest days. My culture is hamburgers, MTV, and iPhones. I'm Mexican by DNA and I'm proud of that, but it doesn't seem right for me to claim something I have no business claiming.

At least that's how I feel. I told Mom that, and she rolled her eyes.

Sorry, mamacita, but that's how I feel.

Also...when it comes to speaking Spanish, I can't roll my Rs very well. When I try, I sound like I'm drowning in phlegm...so that's discouraging.

Where was I?

Oh, right, introducing my family.

Last, but certainly not least, is Jessy. Jessy's fifteen and came to live with us when she was two - her parents died in a car crash, and Dad stepped in to take her without a second thought. Because we were raised together, we're basically sisters; calling her my cousin feels weird, so I'm not going to do it anymore. I'm a goofball and rarely take anything seriously, but protecting and looking out for my sister is a different story. Don't mess with the Jess or you'll get the Alex.

I'm serious. Don't even think about it.

Now, Jess and I are alike in ways, but unalike in others. For one, we both love reading and learning new stuff. On the flip side, she's a little more...let's say...timid than I. Shy, awkward, really self-conscious, you know, a total dweeb. She gets panic attacks sometimes and has trouble breathing and she worries over *everything*.

What if I walk outside and a meteor hits me? Then a marching band stomps me into the pavement? Then a freak rain shower sweeps me away? I better just stay in my room and hide.

She's not that bad, but she might as well be sometimes.

Fortunately for her, she has a brave, bold, *awesome* big sister to give her the kicks in the butt she needs to excel. Without me, she'd probably be a hermit by now.

And smell funny.

Anyhoo, that's enough setup. Now, your feature presentation. I call it *Whoops! I Woke the Dead*.

Muhahahahaha!

CHAPTER ONE

It all started on October 28, a couple days before Halloween – AKA my favorite holiday *ever*. See, I'm a *huge* horror fan and during the rest of the year, that puts me at odds with friends and family. God forbid I put a plastic skull on my nightstand; Jessy will *flip*. *That's really tacky, Alex, you should put it away.* Or *Eww, that's really creepy,* stop. My lunch group at school turns sickly green if I start talking about *The Texas Chainsaw Massacre* (then he put her on a meathook – LOL) and Mom and Dad finger wag because *uuuuh, you're watching horror movies, Alex, uhhh.* But the Halloween season is different. Starting in mid-October, *everyone's* a morbid ghoul. Even Mom and Dad; she'll spend hours sitting at the kitchen table and making decorations, and he'll watch *MonsterFest* on AMC. Don't tell him I said this, but I really cherish kicking my feet up and watching horror movies with my dad - sharing what you love with who you love really hits the spot.

So, October 28: It was a Saturday and I worked the night before so I slept in. Before you say anything, yes, I have a job making pies and pasta at Pissy's Pizza (off-putting name, I know) and I'm super good at it.

Visions of pumpkins and ghosts danced through my head, and in my sleep, I smiled. I went to roll over, and it happened.

I started to fall.

My heart rocketed into my throat and my eyes shot open just as I dropped over the side. My life flashed before me (wow, I was so cool) and I hit the floor with a melodic, dying scream that sounded *nothing* like a cat being murdered. I lay there for a moment, tangled in the blanket and wedged between my bed and the desk, then creaked one eye tentatively open. I'm not dead? *Whew.*

Sitting up, I yawned, gave a big stretch, and stumbled to my feet. Because we live in a tiny, crackerjack ranch house with three bedrooms and Dad *insists* on having an office "for the business", Jess and I share a room. Her half is neat, tidy, and obsessively organized.

Mine is not.

Hey, between working at Pissy's and volunteering at the library, I'm a busy girl, so picking up after myself kinda takes a backseat. Last night, when I shambled into the house past midnight, dead on my feet and covered in dough, I kicked my shoes off, peeled my pants off and dropped into bed. The latter lay in a heap in front of the desk, and the former were five feet apart from one another and facing different directions, like a couple in the midst of giving each other the silent treatment. Getting up, I threw the blanket back on the bed and, in my tank top and underwear, went to the head, scratching my butt as I went.

In the bathroom, I sat on the toilet, propped my elbows on my knees, and rested my face in my hands. Sleep swirled in my head like a raging snowstorm, and I started to nod, but caught myself with a jerk.

On Saturdays, I help Mr. Atkins at the library. Seventy-two and frail with a shock of white hair, glasses, and a mustache, Mr. Atkins was both the town librarian and the curator of the historical society. Dressed perpetually in slacks, a sweater, and a tweed jacket with patches on the elbows (either the coolest outfit ever or the dumbest, I haven't decided yet) he was what you'd call a queer duck if you were a homophobe. For one, he talked to himself, and for another, he talked like a character from a P.G. Wodehouse story ("Splendid! Right-ho!). He reminds me of Doc Brown from *Back to the Future* only less science-y. I might be flippant and carefree and annoying (that last one per Jess), but I'm responsible when I have to be, so calling out and playing sick wasn't an option.

Mr. Atkins needed my help and my help I would render.

Sigh.

Done with my morning pee, I jumped in the shower and turned the water as hot as it would go, because nothing wakes you up like having your skin melted off by boiling water.

After valiantly assisting the aged and infirm antiquarian formerly known as Mr. Atkins, I had work - yay.

Sarcasm.

Today, though, I'd probably get to leave early because my boy Langston worked and he was a machine; really, this dude can do the work of three people and not even break a sweat. He lived, breathed, and slept Pissy's, kind of like SpongeBob with the Krusty Krab...only with Squidward's personality. Strange dude, but cool nevertheless.

As awake as I'd ever be, I cut the spray, jumped out, and toweled off, then put yesterday's undies back on. In my room, I switched them out for a clean pair (never know when you're gonna get lucky, kids, always change your drawers) and dressed in a pair of jeans and a black T-shirt with AC/DC across the front. I freaking *love* AC/DC. In fact, all eighties metal; that stuff rules. Blame my grandfather, because while Dad has lame-o taste in music, *his* dad is lit.

Putting my shoes on, I went into the kitchen. Mom stood at the stove in a threadbare pink robe that was probably older than me, and fried bacon and eggs; Dad sat at the table with the day's issue of *The New York Post*; and Jess-a-less sat across from him, bent over a notebook and writing something. It was either homework or poetry.

Short and petite with clear eyes and her rust-colored hair held back in a perky ponytail that begged to be swatted, she looked like literally none of us; you could tell she didn't fit. Only she did because this is her home and she's my sister, so there.

Dad glanced up from his paper when I came in, faded blue eyes, and sniffed. "It lives."

Giving in to temptation, I flicked Jess's ponytail and dropped into the chair next to her. "Look who's talking. Shouldn't you be at work?"

He *meh*'d. "Fred can handle it."

Fred was his cook, a Vietnam vet who was working there when Dad bought the place in 2014. Because they were both army nerds, they were BFFs and talked about war and stuff. You'd be trying to eat your burger and they'd be at the counter gossiping like a couple of girls about all the severed limbs and bomb-blasted dead people they saw. And he has the audacity to call *me* a ghoul. Dad didn't trust many people, but he trusted Fred and let him open and close by himself. For as much smack Dad talked about not wanting to go in, though, he always did...eventually.

"You're lucky you own the place," I said.

I slouched coolly to the side and draped my arm over the back of the chair. This whole time, Jess hadn't so much as looked up from her project. I craned my neck to look over her shoulder, and coming alive, she crossed her arms over it. "No, stop."

I arched my brow in my best Rock imitation. "Uh...okay."

"It's private."

I held my hands up, palms out. "Okay." Then, to be a jerk, "I'll just read it when you're asleep."

"You'll have to find it first," she said cockily.

"Under your bed, that's where you hide everything."

The color drained from her face, and I smirked. Jess thought she was slick, but you gotta get up pretty early to pull one over on ol' Alex. "I don't hide stuff under there."

Dad watched us over the top of his paper. *You hide stuff? What do you hide? Drugs? Weapons?*

"Yes you do," I said. I started to say *That's where you hid* 50 Shades of Grey, but stopped myself. That might be going a little too far; the embarrassment of Mom and Dad finding out she read something like *that* would probably kill her. She'd probably have a heart attack if she knew *I* knew.

Before she could protest, Mom brought our plates over and set them in front of us. "Here, hide this in your stomachs."

Bacon, toast, eggs, and grits - you don't have to tell *me* twice!

While we ate, Dad divided his attention between his food and the paper, and Jessy covered her mouth with her hand. She has this thing about not liking people looking at her while she eats. Yeah, I know, she's a mess, but I love her.

"I saw Mr. Sloan at the supermarket yesterday," Mom said. The morning sun falling through the window over the sink set her face on fire, and holy wrinkles. She was forty-five but she could easily pass for fifty. Her long black hair, done up in a slack and half-hearted ponytail that lay limp between her shoulder blades, was free of grays, though. I think she dyes it and fronts like she doesn't.

"Yeah?" I asked. "How's he doing?"

"Good. He uses a cane now."

Mr. Sloan was the principal at the elementary school when me and Jess went there…and probably when Mom and Dad went there too. He retired two years ago at eighty-one. I didn't know they let people that old work, but okay.

"Cane?" Dad asked. "You mean bitch stick?"

I snorted laughter and Mom shot him a dirty look. "Will you go to work already?"

"When I'm done." Dad picked up a piece of toast with a flourish and took a mocking bite.

Mom rolled her eyes and shook her head long-sufferingly. With them, it was hard to tell where the kidding ended and the bickering began.

When he was finished, Dad took his plate to the sink, set it in, and leaned over to kiss Mom on the cheek. "Love you."

"Love you too." She turned her head and they kissed full on the lips.

Yuck. There goes *my* appetite.

Just kidding, I was done anyway. I set my plate on top of Dad's and checked the time on my phone. "Gotta go."

"Alright," Mom said. "Be careful."

She always says that when I leave the house like I'm a reckless dope or something. *A busy street? I better cross it without looking both ways, durrr.* "I will."

On my way out, I slapped Jess's ponytail again. "Later, dork."

"Tell Mr. Atkins I said hi."

"I will."

In the living room, a cozy space full of knick-knacks, family photos, and ceramic dolphins (Mom *loves* dolphins), I slipped my coat on and went outside. The morning was bright and cool, the sky cobalt blue and the light that vivid shade of

12

gold you only see in fall. Houses faced the street and the trees along the sidewalk blazed with autumnal color. The tang of burning leaves found my nose, and I drew a deep breath. *Ahhh.* Love that smell.

Pulling my jacket closed against the chill, I went down the steps and hung a left. Next door, Old Man Krause raked fallen leaves in his front yard. "Morning, Mr. Krause," I called.

"Don't talk to me, Warner," he spat without looking up, "I'm busy."

Well then.

I followed West Street to Aldrich, where the houses are bigger and the people slightly richer. Boys rode bikes, girls skipped rope, and a dog trotted aimlessly back and forth, tongue hanging out. He saw me, crossed the street, and sniffed my shoe. "You smell pizza stuff, don't you?" I scratched behind his ears. God only knows what I dropped on it last night.

By way of answering, he licked it.

Shortly, he got bored and wandered off, and I went on my way. Heigh-ho, heigh-ho, off to the li-berry I go. Mispronouncing words triggers Jess's OCD so I do it a lot. Hey, gotta keep her on her toes, right? It's like a form of toughening her up. The uninformed call it bullying, I call it a public service.

Two blocks later, Aldrich filtered into Main Street. Two-story brick buildings lined the way and people moved up and down the sidewalks on Saturday errands. I took a left and crossed town square, a patch of green edging the old county courthouse. A statue of Pickett Meade's most famous native son dominated the commons.

Wilko the White Rapper.

As his name might suggest, he was a white boy who spat lyrics like a Tommy gun spits bullets. He won a bunch of rap battles in Warrenton and Culpepper, then took D.C. by storm. For a while, the press hailed him as the Mid-Atlantic Riff-Raff. He cut a track with Post Malone but got kicked off the Post Malone tour for getting messed up on sizzurp and using the N-word.

With cornrows, grillz, and a bandana tied around his forehead Tupac style, ol' Wilko was *not* the kind of guy you usually see immortalized in bronze, but in a town this small, you take what you can get.

Tragically, Wilko went the way of many rappers when he was gunned down in a drive-by two years ago; the gunmen mistook him for someone more important and lit him up as he came out of a porta-potty in Southeast. He was buried in Westvale Cemetery on the other side of town; his crypt has chrome spinners on it.

The library was housed in an American Foursquare with blue siding and a slate roof. It sat in a grove of trees beyond the railroad tracks, and if you weren't looking for it, you were likely to blow right past. A bush covers the sign out front, which probably throws people off. I offered to trim it, but Mr. Atkins doesn't trust me with power tools.

I climbed the steps and went in through the front door. Straight ahead, a hall led to a kitchen at the back of the house, and to my right, a steep set of narrow stairs provided access to the second floor. The wallpaper was blue with white floral print and the woodwork was scuffed and dull with age. An archway on either side of the foyer opened onto a shadowy parlor crammed with bookshelves. The cinnamon smell of old books seasoned the air and a tranquil hush lay over the house like a blanket of newly-fallen snow.

Mr. Atkins was in his tiny office off the west parlor. When I say tiny, brother, I mean tiny. It was originally a closet before he had the walls knocked down and widened. Stacks of books, loose papers, and filing cabinets towered around the desk, and the only way to *get* to said desk was by a thin little pathway. He held a big magnifying glass to his face and closely studied a ledger by the comfortable glow of a lamp.

Here I am, buddy, notice me.

When he didn't, I said, "Hey, Mr. Atkins."

He started, looked up, and adjusted his glasses. He leaned forward, squinted like he couldn't see me, and then sat back. "Oh, hello, Alex. What brings you by?"

"Uh...I always come in on Saturdays. Remember?"

"Right," he said with a laugh, then shook his head (duh, of course you do). "Forgive me, I was cleaning out the attic last night and I found this book. I've been here reading it ever since."

All-nighter, huh? I know all about those. I once stayed up all night to read one of the *Dark Tower* books. By the end of it, I was a zombie.

"What book?" It takes a special tome to keep a man awake all night.

He picked it up, marked his place with his thumb, and showed me the cover. Not that I could make out the title from here. "*The History and Social Influence of the Potato*."

…

Wow.

Fascinating.

"It's terribly engrossing."

I nodded slowly. "Riveting."

"Very," he said, oblivious to my sarcasm.

Neither one of us spoke for a moment. "So, uh, what do you want me to do?"

He opened his mouth to speak, then closed it again and hummed thoughtfully. "I don't have very much for you today." An idea seemed to then strike him and his eyebrows rose. "You *could* clean out and organize the storeroom in the basement. That way I can continue reading uninterrupted."

Ugh. That storeroom was packed with junk. It'd take me *hours* to clean it.

Oh well. I could get started on it and finish Monday or Tuesday. "Alright," I said heavily.

"Thank you."

Yeah, yeah, yeah. Leaving him to it, I went back through the foyer and down the stairs to the basement. At the bottom, a door bearing a gold plate presented itself: PICKETT'S MEADE TOWN HISTORICAL SOCIETY. I dug my copy of the key from my pocket, unlocked the door, and went inside, snapping the light on as I went.

Most of the space was given over to display cases filled with corroded arrowheads and musket balls people dug out of the ground and brought in.

Framed, black and white photos of Pickett's Meade at various points in history hung on the walls.

The storeroom was off to my right. I opened it, pulled the overhead cord, and deflated. The mess was even worse than I remembered. There were boxes, filing cabinets, chairs, Civil War muskets, and a thousand other pieces of junk heaped haphazardly about.

I blew a puff of air and shrugged out of my jacket. Like Dad says, the longer you stand around moping about something, the longer you'll be there. I tossed my jacket aside, metaphorically rolled my sleeves up, and fell in.

First, I took as much of the crap out as possible and set it aside. Next, I dusted, swept, rearranged things, and hurt my back moving a heavy filing cabinet. What's in here, rocks? When the space was as empty as I could get it, I brought everything back in and carefully packed it all together like a puzzle. Or Jenga blocks, 'cause if you pulled one thing out, the whole mess was coming down house of cards style.

Ah, there, done...for the most part. I dusted my hands and turned around, flush with accomplishment...then stopped.

Whoops.

One more thing.

A metal lock box stared up at me from the floor like Oliver Twist. *Can I have some more, sir?* It was roughly two feet by two feet, rusted, covered in dust, and had a flimsy little lock that wouldn't stop a toddler.

I bent over, picked it up, and went into the storeroom. Literally every spot was taken. Huh. Where oh where am I?

Like the big dumb oaf I totally am not, I kicked a filing cabinet and it started to fall. My heart jolted and I reacted on pure instinct; the lockbox flew from my hands and landed on the floor, and I caught myself on the cabinet.

Darn it.

I brushed my hair out of my eyes and took a deep, resolute breath. Y'know, Mr. Filing Cabinet, I'm here to *help*. The least you can do is not try to kill me.

Sorry, Alex the cabinet seemed to say sheepishly, *it's just been so long since I murdered someone.*

The box lay upside down on the floor. I bent to grab it, but paused. In the fall, the lock snapped off and the lid popped open, freeing what was inside. It sat next to the foot of a broken chair, lonely and forlorn.

Double darn it.

I started to pick it up, but wrenched my hand back with a gasp.

It had a face.

A *human* face.

Heart knocking, I leaned over, and realized it was just a book. A book bound in cracked, skin-colored leather. The face, twisted features and mouth open in a frozen scream of agony, was slightly raised, like an image in a macabre pop-up book. Shadows seethed in its gaping eyes, and...it was just creepy, okay?

And creepy is my middle name.

"Oh, wow," I marveled. I copped a squat, crossed my legs, and picked it up. The leather was warm and fleshy in my hands, almost like the book were *alive*,

Ew. Kinda gross, but okay.

The face regarded me like *I* was the spooky one (*oh no, an Alex – ahhhh!*). I opened it to the first page, yellow and brittle with age. Tight, flowery script marched across the paper in compact, inky columns, and a sketch of a guy being sawed in half occupied the bottom right corner.

Whoa.

There were fifty pages of this stuff. Drawings of people being burned, people being cut up, people getting their hearts ripped out and their brains eaten. I tried to decipher the writing, but in addition to being in cursive (which is hard af to understand), it was in another language...I think. If you asked me, I'd say it was a witch's spellbook and they put it down here after they burned her at the stake. They tried to destroy it, but because of Satanic dark magic, it was indestructible. Burning it didn't work and when they threw it in the lake, it later appeared on one of the witch-killers' nightstands, just chilling like it paid rent. *Hey, how's it goin'?* They finally shoved it in this anti-magic lockbox and hid it down here so no one would ever find it.

Then, along came Alex.

Oh, what dark mysteries it held; what arcane secrets privy to only a few learned scholars.

I don't know what dark, malignant power compelled me to take the book and slip it under my shirt. I blame the devil...and Jessy...everyone but myself.

Closing the box and setting it aside, I shut the door and went back upstairs, holding my stomach like I had the runs. The book felt funny against my belly, and I shivered.

Mr. Atkins was still in his office, still reading about potatoes. Standing there in the doorway, concealing the book beneath my shirt, I felt a twinge of guilt. Oh, come on, I'll bring it back. I just wanna get a better look, okay?

And find out what that writing says.

"I'm done." Could he tell from my voice that I was a thieving a-hole?

"Alright," he said simply, not even glancing up. "See you Monday."

Guess not.

"Okay. Bye."

On the porch I stopped, took the book out, and turned it over in my hands. The binding was stitched together in places and tattered in others.

Is this, uh, real human skin?

Awesome.

Now, I just needed someone to help me read the writing.

And I knew just the person.

Twenty minutes later, after much hoofing, I found Jessy sitting at her desk and writing. Still at it, huh? I went over, perched on the edge, and dropped the book on top of her work station. She recoiled, then, realizing she'd just been Alexized, she took a deep, centering breath.

"Hey, Jess, check it out. It's a spellbook."

She looked up at me with a tight-lipped expression, then to the book. She furrowed her brow and leaned over to get a better look. "Ew!" She crossed her eyes. "Where'd you get it?"

"Found it at the library." I gave her the 411 and her features slowly knotted in shocked disgust. "So," I concluded, "I brought it back here."

She gaped. "You *stole* it?"

I missed a beat. "Well, no, I'm not keeping it, I just -"

Jess cut me off. "Did you ask permission?"

"..."

"So you stole it."

I sighed. "Okay, technically, yes, I *stole* it." Here I whipped out some air quotes. "But in spirit, I only borrowed it."

Jess threw her head back and moaned. "Alex, why?"

"Because." I leaned over and opened the cover. "Look, it's really old. Like Mom and Dad. You'll love it."

She eyed the page warily. She was a history geek *and* a book lover, so she couldn't pass this up even if she wanted to.

Anxiously biting her lower lip, she gave in to her curiosity.

Ha, check and mate.

"What's it say?" I asked. "It's a spellbook, right?"

Jess scanned the words and muttered to herself. "Yes," she said absently. "It says, *He who owns this booke shall weeld the power of the infernal one...*" she trailed off and looked like she was going to be sick. "I don't like this," she said quickly and snapped the cover closed.

The infernal one?

As in…Satan himself?

Cool.

I picked the book up, set it in my lap, and opened it. "Didja see all the cool pictures? There's one of a guy getting mauled by a cat. Like, hello, how do you lose to a cat? It's five pounds and twenty inches tall." I laughed and shook my head. Good times, good times.

Jess hugged herself.

"You cold, Jess?"

"No." She glared at the book. "That...thing. Get it away. It's awful."

I snorted. "Yeah. Awfully awesome."

"It's gross and yuck and evil."

Evil? Uh, since when did my sister become superstitious? "Oh, it's not evil; it's just a book."

"A book full of evil."

I rolled my eyes. "Jess -"

"I'm serious," she said firmly. "Get it away from me or I'm telling."

Oh.

She *was* serious.

Softening my tone, I said, "Look, you don't really believe that stuff, do you?"

Jess wrapped her arms around herself like a girl in a straight jacket. "No, I don't, but it gives me the creeps. Take it back where you found it."

I sighed. Her mind was made up. I stood. "Fine, I'll take it away."

"Thank you."

WHOOPS I WOKE THE DEAD

I couldn't take it back to the library since I had to go to work. By the time I got home, it'd be closed, and it wasn't open on Sundays, so that left me high and dry until Monday. In the meantime, I hid it in the linen closet between two ugly sheet sets no one ever used, then checked my phone. Did I have time to take a shower and wash all the dust and yuck from the storeroom off?

Nope.

Oh well.

I grabbed my uniform, went into the bathroom, and hurriedly changed. Black pants, maroon shirt with PISSY's over the left breast in white, and a black, Jamie Kennedy tier sun visor that made me look almost as dorky as my dad.

Pissy's, the best pizza place to ever live, was on the edge of Main two blocks from the trestle bridge that carries the street across the Pickett River. It sits on a corner apart from everything else. The dining room is microscopic (two booths and a counter), and the kitchen is so narrow it makes racist comments. My boy Langston stood behind the register with a blank expression. Tall with a little bit of chub and messy blonde hair, Langston had two modes: Leave me alone and kill me now. He loved making pizza, but he simply tolerated everything else. His voice was flat, his eyes sleepy, and his shoulders stooped; he looked like a slacker but trust me, guy's not.

"What up, Lang?" I grabbed my apron from the stand by the counter.

"Hey," he mumbled.

Langston loves crafting quality pies, but you know what *else* he likes? Bruce Lee. Dude is *obsessed* with Bruce Lee. He even has a tattoo of Bruce's face on his back.

I only know all this because one time this guy in a ski mask tried to rob us, and while I cowered behind the counter (*I'm gonna die!!),* Langston just stood there, gun in his face. *Sir,* he said, *please leave.*

When the guy didn't, Langston grabbed his arm, snapped it in two, and hit him with a sick throat punch that took the doctors, like, five surgeries to fix. Later, I asked him how he did it, and he said he learned from his idol...Bruce Lee.

"Ready for the big Halloween party?" I asked.

Every year, Alton and Margaret Brenner, the richest people in town, threw a huge costume party at their McMansion on Pine Street.

"I didn't get an invite," he said.

Oh. "Well...it's open to everyone."

"I don't go anywhere unless I'm invited."

Like a vampire – lol. "Alright, well...wanna come to the big Halloween party?"

"No. I work that night."

I sputtered. "On Halloween?"

God, I couldn't imagine working and missing the best and most important holiday in the world. I'd probably cry the entire time.

"Yes. I need extra hours."

I parked my butt on the counter next to him and planted my hands on either side of me, legs kicking back and forth. "Why's that?"

Langston didn't speak for a moment, and I started thinking he wasn't going to tell me. *Go away, Alex, you're bugging me.* He's totally said that before, btw. "I'm saving up so I can fly to

California, find Quentin Tarantino and spit in his face."

Ah. Quentin Tarantino, the guy who made *Once Upon a Time...In Hollywood.* Langston hated that movie because it made Bruce Lee look like, "A stupid asshole." When it came out, he railed about it for almost a month. I assumed he moved on but apparently not.

"Pretty sure that constitutes assault."

"I don't care," Langston deadpanned.

Alrighty.

Jumping off the counter, I made my way to the time clock, punched my card, and went back into the kitchen. Pat, the manager, stood next to the oven and wrung his hands like a Bond villain plotting world domination.

Ugh. I was hoping he wouldn't be here today. "Hey, Pat," I said, fighting to keep the disdain from my voice.

Pat whipped his head up like Gollum and flashed a big, fevered smile. "Hello, Alex."

A short, fat troll of a man with greasy black hair that veiled his weasel eyes, endlessly oozing pimples, and a snout in place of a nose, Pat was the kind of manager who delighted in throwing his weight around. The technical term is power-tripping asshole, I think. He lived in his mom's basement (literally) and rode an electric scooter to work (scooters are lame, sorry not sorry). On his off-time, he drew art for a cartoon fandom. He brought some of it in to show off one day, and it was shockingly good...but contained just a *little* more incest than I expected. *And this is Lemy fucking his sister Lyra.*

Everyone gasped.

Even Langston.

Twenty-eight or twenty-nine, Pat was always staring at my butt and boobs like a grade-A perv, and just being around him made me feel dirty, like every part of my body was lightly coated in slime.

I washed my hands in the sink, then grabbed a wad of paper towels. The entire time, Pat watched me through his bangs, the tip of his tongue swiping his crooked, yellow teeth. A shiver went down my spine and I noped out. In the dining room, I leaned against the counter next to Langston. "Slow day, huh?"

"Pretty much."

No sooner had I said that, two guys came in the door. I stood up straight - look alive, Warner - and opened my mouth to greet them.

When I saw who it was, my heart fluttered.

Tim and his cousin Mark walked up to the counter. Tim's my boyfriend (<3). Short and slight with brown hair and cute little glasses, he was hot, dorky, and always let me win at video games.

That, ladies and gentlemen, is what I call a keeper.

Mark, it just so happened, was Jessy's boyfriend. He looks like that dude from *My Friend Dahmer*: Tall; shaggy blonde hair; painfully scrawny. With his hooked nose and beady little eyes, he resembled a bird too (caw, caw, your date's here, Jess). He has mild Asperger's, which makes him: 1) flat and unexpressive; and 2) socially uninhibited. Honestly, guy doesn't feel shame about anything. If his wiener popped out in front of everyone, he'd just go *oops* and tuck it back in. If that happened to *me,* I'd curl up in a little ball and die from the humiliation. He also can't read social cues. He told me he once spent an entire day thinking a girl liked him only to find out she hated his guts. *I didn't see that one coming,* he said.

Propping my elbow on the counter, I set my chin in my hand and batted my eyelashes at Tim. He's so dreamy.

Watch how a girl in love greets her beau.

"Hey, short shit, how's the weather down there?"

He leaned against the edge and wiggled his eyebrows. "Hot and steamy."

"You should use Tinactin for that. I think that cures jock itch."

Langston sighed, probably annoyed by our interplay.

"Why do that when I can have you scratch it for me?" Tim asked smoothly.

I shrugged. "Alright. Let me grab my tweezers."

He opened his mouth then shut it again. At a loss for words. Ha, Alex Warner, knockin' 'em speechless since 2005. "It's not *that* small," he finally said.

"Uh-uh, that's what they all say. What do you want?"

He glanced up at the menu. "Uh...just a large cheese pizza and an order of wings."

I rang him up, took his money, and shoved it into the register while Langston wandered off to start the pizza and wings. "Anything cool going on?" I asked. Mark was currently pacing the dining room and inspecting the floor and walls like his name was OSHA.

"Nah, not really. We're just hanging at my place."

"There's a cobweb," Mark piped up. He jutted his chin to the corner behind the door.

Reaching under the counter, I grabbed a dry microfiber cloth, balled it up, and threw it at him. "He who sees it gets to clean it."

He stared at me, then the cloth, then grabbed it, got down on his knees and swatted the web away.

I was just kidding, but okay. Less work for me! "What are you guys doing?"

"Playing GTA 5."

"Lucky." GTA 5 is my all-time favorite game. The shooting and blowing stuff up is pretty dope, but I'm more in it for the open world aspect. Freeways, country roads, all sorts of towns and mountains to explore – it's *awesome*.

Tim grabbed a carry-out menu and glanced it over. "What time do you get off? You can come over. Just be warned, my folks are there."

He said that like I was going to try and jump his bones or something. I really like you Tim, but no, I'm not really for all *that* right now. He knew that and he respected it. Honestly, I think he's as nervous over it as I am. One time, we were playing Xbox and I went to reach over his lap for some chips, and he screamed, grabbed his crotch, and crossed his legs. He tried to play it off like his back twinged (*gee, that really hurt*) but I'm pretty sure he thought I was going for his junk.

"Too late to hang," I said with a sigh. "Maybe tomorrow."

Tim winced. *Oooh, no good.* "We're going to see my grandma tomorrow."

Darn. "Monday?"

"Well, yeah, I can't miss school."

Boy, that was the truth. Tim's a smart cookie but he has trouble applying himself in math and science (just like me) and grade-wise, he walked a slippery slope. One wrong move and he was going down like a fat kid tripping on his shoelaces.

Shortly, Langston came out with a pizza box and a Styrofoam container of wings and handed them across the counter. "I'll see you later," Tim said.

"Alright." I didn't want him to leave but, alas, he had to.

"Tell Jessy I said hi," Mark said.

"Why not text her?"

Mark didn't miss a beat. "Because it means more in person, even if it *is* coming secondhand."

Can't argue with him there.

When they were gone, I slumped against the counter. "Is it time to go home yet?"

"No," Langston said.

Ugh.

Having to work for a living sucks.

You know what sucks even more? When your bully of a manager comes in, says, "If you got time to lean, you got time to clean," and makes you scrub the grease off the vent hoods.

That sucks *quite* a bit more.

CHAPTER TWO

Mondays, believe it or not, are one of my easier days. I'm off Sunday and usually collapse from the week's accumulated exhaustion before ten. I wake the next morning at six bright-eyed and bushy-tailed and for a few hours (until math spoils my mood), anything is possible. October 30, I woke to the sound of rain ten minutes before my alarm was set to go off. Jessy was already up and dressed in a sweater and slacks. Get this: She was folding laundry. "What are you doing?" I asked and sat up.

"Putting my clothes away." She said it like folding laundry at 5:50am was the most normal thing in the world.

"This early?"

"Yes, this early," Jess shot back. She scanned the room and frowned. "And before we leave, you need to pick up the yuck you call your half of the room."

Pfft. Yuck? Why, there's not even -

Clothes, shoes, and dirty underwear were strewn across the floor.

Oh.

I could have *sworn* I cleaned this up yesterday. "Fine," I said and flopped my head back against the pillow. My motivation tanked and suddenly, anything *wasn't* possible.

Jess finished up and sailed out of the room, and I sat up again. Might as well get this over with.

I hurriedly picked up my clothes, crammed them into my overflowing hamper, and dressed in jeans and a black hoodie over a white T-shirt. Water streaked the window pane and hissed in the street; it was going to be a long walk to school.

Unless...

I grabbed my bookbag and went into the kitchen. Jess leaned against the counter and munched sparingly on a granola bar like a cute woodland critter, and Dad sat at the table with the *Post* in front of his face. "Hey," I said and sat across from him, "you're looking less lame than usual today."

He regarded me suspiciously over the top of the paper, braced for anything. "What do you want?"

"A ride to school." I smiled prettily.

Instead of *sure, Alex, whatever you want, hun,* he stared daggers at me, and I started to squirm. "Yeah," he said wryly, "because I was totally going to let my teenage daughters walk in the pouring rain. That's exactly something I'd do. Glad you think so highly of me."

Aaaand here we go. "Nevermind, I'd rather walk."

I started to get up but he stopped me. "Leave the house without me and you're grounded." The twinkle in his eye told me he was playing, but I didn't wanna take any chances. Tomorrow was

Halloween and I was *not* going to risk missing it. "You're the boss," I said and parked my butt.

"Actually, your mom's the boss," he said and snapped the paper with a flourish. "I'm just middle management."

Hey, like Pat. "No wonder you throw your weight around." I leaned back in my chair. "It's always the lowest guy in the power structure who abuses his power."

Dad snorted. "What dumbass told you that?"

"You."

He didn't say anything to *that*.

Since I had some time to spare, I decided to have a spot of breakfast. "Hey, Jess," I said over my shoulder, "throw me one of those granola bars, will you?"

Jessy swallowed. "Get it yourself."

"Oh, come on." I put on my saddest puppy dog face.

"Nope, not falling for it."

Darn. I had to bring out the big guns. Thrusting out my bottom lip, I worked up just enough tears to sparkle. "B-But sisters…"

She darted her eyes to me then away, her jaw clenching with determination. *I won't cave this time*, her expression said. She made the grave mistake of meeting my gaze, and I quivered my lip. *Pweeze.*

Sighing, she broke like a fat guy's diet, went to the pantry, and grabbed a bar. She tossed it underhand, and leaning to the side, I snatched it. My left butt cheek started to slip, and my balance upset. With a high, wavering *Whoa*, I tipped, but threw out my arm and slapped my hand on the floor at the last second, saving myself from certain death. "Nice throw, but I gotta deduct points 'cause that landing was a *little* shaky."

"That's your fault."

"No, it's yours." I ripped open the wrapper. "The thrower is responsible for how the catcher catches. Didn't you know? It's, like, a rule of every sport."

Dad snorted. "You're full of it."

"Yeah, full of knowledge."

Jess rolled her eyes and left the room, probably to do a quick dust, mop, and vacuum before we left, and I dug into my bar. It had dried cranberries in it. Yuuum.

Across from me, Dad went through the motions of his daily morning ritual.

Turns page: "Damn liberals."

Turns next page: "Damn conservatives."

It happens like this every day. "Don't you like anyone?" I asked, spraying food.

"I like your mom."

I-I couldn't tell if he was being serious or insulting me. But you usually can't with him. "She's not a politician."

"That's why I like her."

When he was done bellyaching about Republicans and Democrats, we piled into his 2009 Focus and lit out for school, Jess in the back and me riding shotgun. Oldest *always* gets shotgun, even if the youngest calls it. Dirty rainwater sluiced through the gutters, carrying leaves and twigs into dark, open drains (*we all float down here, Jess*).

Dad turned onto Schoolhouse Road and braked to let an old woman pushing a cart pass. A half mile later, Pickett's Meade High appeared from the mist like a ship at sea. A big, blocky, ugly ship with a covered breezeway, a courtyard, and a higher-than-usual dropout rate. Kids streamed from buses idling at the curb, and Principal Rader and Vice Principal Wuornos stood by the door, glaring at their charges like a couple of serial killers. He was balding with glasses, and she butt ugly with blonde hair. I call them "the gruesome twosome." Mom calls them something a wee bit stronger that starts with an "A" and ends with "ssholes."

That's, like, the one thing we agree on.

Pulling over, Dad put the car in park, and Jess flung her door open. "Bye," she said and climbed out.

"Bye," Dad replied.

I started to get out too.

"Hey."

I looked at him, and for a moment we stared each other down like two gunslingers getting ready to draw. Then, he tapped his cheek.

Where I come from, that means *Free shot,* so I knocked his ass out and left.

Not really. I leaned in and kissed his cheek. "There," he said.

"Love you."

"Love you too."

Getting out into the damp chill, I flipped my hood up, grabbed my backpack, and hurried across the street. Inside the main lobby, the floor was slick and peppered with dead leaves. The office was to the right behind a glass partition and the gym was to the left, its doors standing open. A hallway lined with lockers stretched to the cafeteria, and a cross hall ran east to west from one end of the building to the other. At my locker, I put in the combination (39-42-56) and grabbed my history book.

I slammed the door just as my bestie Kyra walked up. Kyra's a VSCO girl, which is like a Valley Girl mixed with a vegan...I think. She wears oversized T-shirts, scrunchies around both wrists, flip-flops in every weather (except snow), and rocks a puka shell choker. I know, I know, I'm embarrassed to be seen with her too sometimes, but we've known each other since kindergarten. I wasn't as awesome back then and my first day I was really nervous. Kyra noticed and asked me to play with her during playtime, and we've been best friends through it all.

"Hey," she said and opened her locker. Her voice was perky, upbeat, and, not gonna lie, annoying. Today she wore a gray T-shirt that almost reached her knees, flipper-floppers, and her dirty blonde hair in a messy bun that sat on top of her head like a giant spider.

"Hey," I said, trying really hard not to stare at it but staring anyway.

She took a drink from her hydro flask (lime green, yuck) and exchanged it for her science book. "Ready for the big math test?"

Ugh.

I forgot about *that*.

"No," I said and hung my head.

"That's okay, I *totes* believe in you." She glanced down at my hand, and her neck muscles started to strain like that guy in the meme.

Uh-oh.

"No," I forestalled.

Her face turned red.

"Not happening."

"Just one, okay?" she begged.

I dunno if all VSCO girls do this, but Kyra gives scrunchies and metal straws to *everyone*. She's like Johnny Appleseed or something (heh, Johnny VSCOseed. I gotta write that down). If she spotted a naked wrist, her VSCO senses tingled and she wouldn't be happy until it was clothed in a "totes cute" scrunchie. Oh, and God help you if she saw you drinking out of a plastic bottle. *Ohmigod, that's* really *bad for the environment. Here, have a hydro flask. Save the turtles.*

"No," I said. "I'm not a VSCO girl, I'm an Alex girl."

She threw her head back. "But I have one that will look *so* cute on you." She reached into her gigantic tote bag (with SAVE THE WHALES embroidered across the front), and I took the opportunity to escape. I can be pretty quick when I wanna be.

If you've ever been to high school you know what it's like, so I'll spare you all the boring details. At lunch, I stood in line, got my tray, and sat across from Kyra and her friends, Valerie and Harper. The former was black and the latter a tall, prissy blonde who was a lot more chill than she seemed. They were talking about the Brenners' Halloween party when I rolled up, and I jumped right in. "I can't wait. You guys know what you're going to be?"

Valerie beamed. "I'm going to be a slutty nurse."

Yuck. Okay.

"I'm going to be a slutty clown," Harper said.

Okay, hold up. "A slutty clown?" I asked. "H-How do you do that?"

Preening like it was her time to shine, she said, "You wear makeup, a big red nose...and not much else."

Kyra covered her hand to stifle her VSCO giggle. "Skskksks."

"No, no, I get the concept, but clowns aren't sexy. You'll look dumb."

Her jaw *dropped*. "No, I won't."

"Yes you will."

"No, I won't." She upended her hydro flask and sighed (ahhh, refreshing). "What are *you* going as?"

Even though I haven't mentioned it once in this story, I put a *lot* of thought into my costume. Last year, I went as Gene Simmons from KISS, complete with cape, make-up, and platform boots. This time around, I wanted something a little simpler. "A witch."

"A slutty witch?" Harper asked.

"No, a normal witch."

Harper nodded patronizingly. "Oh."

Yeah, wow, Alex isn't dressing like a thot, what a loser, right? You know, it might not be hip to say this, but I think women and girls should accentuate their minds and personalities instead of their bodies. I mean, I get wanting to be pretty, but

I see girls wearing shorts so tiny the bottoms of their butt cheeks literally hang out. *Oh, but it's hot.* Yeah, I get hot too but I wear normal shorts like a normal person. If you wanna dress that way, fine, but *I* personally think walking around like a mobile meat market with something to sell is objectifying.

I didn't want to be a stick-in-the-mud like my mom, so I didn't say any of that; I just blew a raspberry and waved them off.

Across the cafeteria, Tim waited in line. Ooooh, QT at nine' o'clock. Elsewhere, Jessy and Mark sat across from each other, Jessy smiling and prattling about something lame, no doubt.

Tim got his tray and came over, and my heart fluttered. It always does when I see him. "Hey," I said.

"Hey." He sat next to me and we kissed. Not with tongue, though. We do that sometimes but not in public. "You look nice today."

In jeans, a hoodie, and red Chuck Taylor All-Stars, I looked like I always did...but I blushed anyway. "Thanks – you too."

Kyra, Valerie, and literally everything else faded away until Tim was the only thing left in the world - soft brown eyes, cocky smile, cute dimples. In my native tongue, we call guys like him muy kaleintay.

"I missed you," he said.

He took my hand and threaded our fingers together. "I missed you too." How'd you do on that math test?"

"Good," he said. "I think."

Tim's dad owns an auto body shop (did I already mention that?) and Tim helps him out in the afternoons, so he uses a lot of math.

"You?" Tim asked.

I laughed. "I bombed."

"Really?"

"Nah, I did okay." I took his roll off his tray and took a bite. He cocked an admonishing brow and I giggled like a little girl. "What?"

"I was going to eat that."

"So?"

"Now I don't have one."

"Tough shit."

He pursed his lips and nodded to himself. *I should have seen* that *coming.* Since I'm not a monster, I broke off a piece and shoved it into his mouth; his cheeks puffed out like a squirrel and he gagged.

Pfft. Lightweight.

Ten minutes later, the bell rang and we were forced to part. I know it's *really* early to say something like this, but being around Tim, I get why people marry each other. I used to think it was a formality couples underwent just because, but now I see it for what it is. You marry your best guy (or girl) because when you aren't with them, you aren't complete. Your heart and soul cry out for them and you're dazed and out of sorts until they come back. I'm not saying I'll marry Tim one day (I'm only sixteen and we've been together, like, six months), but, you know...maybe.

Possibly.

Head in the clouds, I went to my next class, totally unaware that in just twenty-four hours my life was going to be thrown into chaos.

CHAPTER THREE

Tuesday, October 31 dawned clear, bright, and a wee bit nipply. The previous night, me, Dad, and Jess stayed up watching Halloween movies on AMC - me munching popcorn and Jess peeking through her fingers because *uhhh, horror movies scare me, uhhh*. Jess, God love her, is the biggest baby in the world when it comes to stuff like that. When she was a little girl, *Monster House* scared the bejesus out of her, and she could barely make it through *Mostly Ghostly: Who Let the Ghosts Out?* In an effort to put some hair on her chest, as Dad might say, I make her watch scary movies with me sometimes. We saw *Get Out* in the Palace Theater downtown, and I'm proud to say she only cowered for *half* of it.

Progress!

Anyway, I got up with my alarm - giddy like a kid on Christmas - caught a shower, and went into the kitchen. Mom, dressed in a gray shirt and a matching blazer over a white blouse, stood at the counter pouring sugar into a cup of coffee. Her hair was pulled back in a lametastic bun and when she glanced at me her eyes were hazy and unfocused with fatigue. "Morning," I sang and grabbed a mug from the drying rack.

"Morning." She brought the cup to her lips, blew away a curl of steam, and took a tentative sip. "Is that your costume?"

I grinned. "Yeah, part of it."

'Part of it' was a long black dress with a ragged hem on top of my normal clothes. Last night after dinner, I drilled a hole in a plastic skull and threaded twine through it; it hung around my neck like a morbid piece of bling. My witch hat was sitting on my dresser.

Mom hummed judgmentally.

"What?" I asked.

"Nothing, I just expected something a little more…" she waved her hands. "Elaborate."

I added cream and sugar. "Eh, I wanted to get back to basics this year."

After she was gone, I finished my coffee and went to get my hat. Jessy stood in front of the full length mirror on the back of the closet door and looked at her reflection over her shoulder. Dressed in a skirt and blazer much like Mom's, she wore glasses (with no lenses because she'd be blinded otherwise) and her hair in a pragmatic bun. Also like Mom's.

Can you guess what she was supposed to be?

"Hey, Teach," I said and grabbed my hat.

Last night, Jess and I carved jack-o'-lanterns at the kitchen table. Mine sat on my nightstand, the candle within filling it with flickering light.

Yes, I slept with a lit pumpkin on my nightstand last night. I also put my earbuds in and listened to my Halloween playlist on my phone. *They're Coming to Take Me Away, haha, hoo hoo, hee hee.*

Like I said, I'm a pretty big Halloween buff.

I dropped onto the edge of the bed and blew out the candle. "How are people going to know you're supposed to be a teacher?" I asked.

Jess, still studying herself, said, "I have an apple."

"So?"

"Teachers eat apples."

"So do librarians. You could easily pass for one of those."

Done, Jess sat at her desk and pulled her heels on. "True, but I think people will get it."

Hmmm. I dunno; people can be kinda dense.

An idea struck me, and I reached into my nightstand and grabbed something. "I got just the thing." I went over to her.

"What?" Jess asked.

I held it up.

A Number 2 pencil. "This." I bent over, and Jess stiffened. I jammed the end lengthwise through her bun, wiggled it to make sure it was stuck fast, and stepped back to admire my handiwork. "There."

Jess turned her head side to side, and the pencil stayed. "How do I look?"

Maybe it was my imagination, but she sounded anxious, like a little girl worrying over her first day of school. My maternal instincts triggered and the urge to sweep my baby sister into the biggest, beariest hug ever came over me. *Shhh, there, there, Jess.* "You look great; in fact...you look as awesome as *me*."

Jess laughed. "I doubt I look *that* awesome."

"Sure you do," I pinched her cheek, "Alex Jr."

She pulled away, laughed, and swatted my hand. "Stop! That hurts."

"Oh, you'll live." I pulled my hat on and grabbed my backpack. "Now come on."

Outside, a needling breeze washed over us and I shuddered. I considered going back in for my jacket, but if I covered up my costume, people wouldn't get the full effect. Sometimes, you gotta suffer for your art.

Wind blew sheets of leaves across the street, and the swaying trees whispered dark secrets to each other…or maybe juicy gossip. I dunno. I speak tree like I speak Spanish.

"You're coming to the party tonight, right?"

Jess, thumbs thrust through the straps of her backpack like a dork, hunched against the wind, her cheeks already red from the cold. "I don't know – crowds."

"Make you nervous, I know. You handle school, though."

She shrugged one shoulder. "That's different. And…I really don't want to be around alcohol or anything, so probably not."

"Jess, there's not going to be any booze there. It's a community party. I don't even think booze is allowed."

She scrunched her lips in thought.

"You should come." I batted my eyelashes like the evil temptress I am. "You can hang out with Mark."

"I don't know. I'll think about it."

We turned onto Schoolhouse Road. The trees here burned like torches and awesome fall decorations adorned all the houses along the way:

Jack-o'-lanterns; blushing, happy scarecrows; plastic skeletons dangling from branches like condemned men hanged by the state; a crooked row of foam gravestones marched across someone's lawn here; and fake spider webs fluttered in the boughs of a big pine.

"You'll have fun; I promise."

"Maybe."

C'mon, Jess, have I ever lied to you?

Actually, don't answer that. I get the feeling that I may have. Once or twice.

In the lobby, Jess went left and I went right; I grabbed my things from my locker. Kyra stood next to hers with her iPhone glued to her ear.

"Ohmigod, like, totally. I have given that girl *so* many scrunchies. I think she keeps losing them." Her eyes went to my bare wrist and her pupils dilated like a shark scenting blood.

See ya.

In class, I sat in my normal spot at the very back of the room (I can still be a good noodle from back here, guys, I swear) and stared at the trees through the window. Girlish excitement crackled through me and sitting still was muy difficulto (adding 'O' to the end of a word automatically makes it Spanish, didn't you know?). In just a few hours, I'd be at the party bobbing for apples, eating candy, jumping out of dark corners and scaring Jess silly...ahhh, I couldn't wait.

At lunch, I dropped into an empty seat next to Tim and nudged him in the ribs with my elbow. "Hey, dork."

He grimaced in pain and rubbed his side. "Oh, I didn't even do it that hard; stop being a baby."

"Felt like a gunshot," he said.

"You're just weak," I dismissed.

"You're just bony."

"You're a sissy." I grinned. "You lack testicular fortitude."

He looked at me.

I looked at him.

Then we laughed.

"Testicular fortitude, huh?" he asked and opened his milk. "I've never heard that one."

LOL. "I know."

He sighed like a gullible goof realizing he just walked into another prank and took a long drink to buy himself some time. "Your mother," he said.

"Oooh, low blow," I said and picked up my fork. "That means you got nothing better, therefore I win."

"Whatever," he said.

See, in case you haven't noticed, coming up with snappy barbs is one of the many, many, *many* things I'm good at. Everyone around me knows that if they step up, they'll get smacked down again, so they rarely even try.

Tim carved a piece of mystery meat with his fork and I impaled a couple of anemic green beans on mine. School food is the only food I don't like. I mean, I eat it though, but it's still gross. Ugh. I swear they eat better in prison. "What time should I pick you up?" Tim asked around a mouthful.

"Party starts at seven and I like to be fashionably late, so we should probably get there at 7:01."

"Okay, SpongeBob," he snorted. "Is Jess coming?"

I looked around and spied Jess-the-bess sitting with Mark and a few of her geeky friends. Mark said something, and she covered her mouth to hide her mushy-gushy giggle. Ahh, how fast they grow up; I remember a time when she thought boys were "yuck" and infested with bugs. Come to think of it, I'm the one who told her that. "I dunno, she was kinda waffling earlier. She thinks the place is gonna be full of drugs, beer, and sex."

That made Tim laugh. Seriously, being a community party, things were generally kept PG. Maybe people did things there but not, like, out in the open. "She's a dweeb."

And *that* earned him another shot to the guts. The air left him in a gasp and he bared his teeth in pain. "Shut up, asshole. My sister's not a dweeb."

"God, I was playing," he cried.

"You don't play with an Alex's Jessy. Bad things happen." I widened my eyes to communicate the severity of my warning. "Bad, *bad* things."

He held one hand up. "Okay, sorry."

The bell rang a few minutes later, and I scarfed down the rest of my lunch. "So, pick up at seven?" Tim asked.

"Yeah, seven's fine."

"Alright." We kissed, then I took my tray to the window and went to science class.

That last half of the day went by s l o w l y, and when the last bell rang at 2:45, I jumped up, shouldered everyone out the way, and raced into the hall.

Halloween party, here I come!

"Maybe I shouldn't." Jess sat at her desk and ran her hair anxiously through her hands like a girl milking a cow. In the light of the lamp, her face was craggy and drawn, like going to a Halloween party was the most stressful thing ever.

She'd been sitting at her desk for nearly an hour fretting over every little thing and every freak possibility (*what if someone's smoking the devil's lettuce, I breathe a little in, and I get "high"? Huh? What then, Alex? What then???*). I sat on my bed with my legs crossed and threw a handful of M&M's into my mouth. "Will you relax, Jess? We're gonna bob for apples, have a cake walk, and eat yummy snacks. That's it."

Though I looked cool and unaffected on the outside (as I am wont to do), I had my own problems. Namely my costume. Maybe it was a little *too* simple. I had a hat, a black dress, and a skull necklace. Understatement is *not* the Alex Warner way, and I was a blasted fool to think I could pull it off. I needed *something* to bring it all together, but what? A broom? Nah, that was too basic. A hydro flask?

"...that's all," Jess was saying.

Whoops, you were talking? I had no clue what she said, so I wung it. Or maybe that's winged it. "Just calm your bits, Jess. I swear, sometimes I think you *like* spagging out."

Jess shot me a dirty look. "Trust me, I don't, but this can go wrong a million different ways. What if someone's drinking or doing drugs and the police come? What if someone spills a beer on us and the cops smell it and think *we* were drinking?

Huh? We'll go to jail and Uncle Kevin and Auntie Maria will be disappointed in us." She caught her breath and turned away, stroking her hair faster and harder. "So, so disappointed."

This girl is so, so difficult. "That's not going to happen," I said with strained patience, "and if by some universal gymnastics it *does*, you have a reputation as a good-girl-slash-teacher's-pet. Mom and Dad will believe you."

She pursed her lips in thought. I softened my tone. "Really, we're gonna have a great time."

For a moment, she gazed into space, her mind working, then she drew a heavy sigh and nodded. "Okay."

"Atta girl." It was 6:28 by the clock on the nightstand and I still didn't have anything to tie my costume together. Sigh. Guess I'll be an unorganized mess. "I'm gonna hit the showers," I said and got up. I might be a mess but at least I'd smell good. My bf was going to be there and I had to be fresh and alluring; can't do that reeking like pits and feet.

Getting up, I grabbed my towel and went out into the hall. Speaking of bad smells, what's that stench? I sniffed the air and gagged. Ugh, it's like mold and mildew and unwashed butt. I looked around, didn't see the source, then surreptitiously took a whiff of my underarms. Do I offend? Nope.

Huh.

Then I smelled my towel.

And threw up in my mouth. Just a little bit.

Ew, when's the last time I switched this bad boy out? I wracked my brain but couldn't remember. Eh. I tossed it aside and went to the linen closet for a new one. I grabbed one, and jumped back in alarm.

There was a face under it.

What the -?

Then I remembered. Oh, the cool, creepy spellbook that creeped Jess out so bad she banished it from our room.

It called my name, and in an instant, I knew I found the thing to make my costume pop.

Covering it with another towel, I went to the bathroom and hopped in the shower. I totally meant to take the book back to the library on Monday but, hey, with me, if it's out of sight it's likely out of mind. Good thing I didn't. Hooray for forgetting.

When I was done, I got out, dried off, and got dressed. I grabbed the book on my way back to the room, and the warm, pulpy feel of it made me cringe. It hummed silently in my hand like a transformer box, and my step faltered. Oooh, that's new. It didn't do this on Saturday.

But of course it'd tremble with unholy life now. It *was* Halloween, after all.

Shudder.

Maybe Jess was right about this thing.

Nah! She's a dweeb with an anxiety disorder, what did she know?

I tucked the book up under my arm, went into the room, and dropped onto my bed. Jess was still at the desk, facing the mirror and putting her hair back in the super duper teacher bun; a metal pin jutted from her mouth like a crack pipe and I tsked. Such a shame to see a good girl go bad. Her future was sooo bright.

6:45. Fifteen minutes until Tim was here...fifteen minutes until he was *supposed* to be here, that is. You know how girls say they'll be ready in five but you're still waiting three hours later? Yeah, guys do that too, only their line is *I'll be there in ten minutes.* A week later they roll up like nothing happened.

Fifteen minutes...guess that gives me time to read.

I cracked the book open and scanned the first page. Jess said this was in English but it was Greek to me. Maybe if Pickett's Meade taught its students CURSIVE WRITING like a normal school system, but noooo. It's "useless" the PTA said. "It has no place in a modern curriculum," they said.

Whatever, I'll just look at the pictures.

Turning the page, I leafed through and stopped at the end. On the inside cover, a column headed OWNERS OF THE BOOKE listed a dozen names, each followed by a date. The first one was 1543.

My jaw dropped.

There was *no way* this book was that old. I can see a hundred years, *maybe* two, but five hundred????

Heh. That dark magic really keeps it, huh?

The last name was Ellie Rimbaugh and per the date beside her name, she took possession of the book in 1743. That's before America was even America, for those of you keeping score at home. We were still British and much of the country was a vast, untapped wilderness filled with Indian tribes, French fur trappers, and limitless natural resources. The Revolution was still thirty years away and we wouldn't gain our independence for forty. Visions of pantaloons, silver buckle slippers, quaint cottages, and Colonial architecture swirled around me and I drew a nostalgic sigh. Yep, those were the days.

Wait, what I am talking about? No they weren't.

A thousand questions occurred to me as I stared down at those names. Who were they? Were they members of the same family? Did they have a coven? How was the book passed down?

I don't know about you, but when *I* have a question, I go to Google. I whipped my phone out and typed ELLIE RIMBAUGH into the search bar, then hit the magnifying glass.

The first result:

ELLIE RIMBAUGH - WIKIPEDIA.

Gasp.

She has her own Wiki page!

You know someone's a heavy hitter when they have their own entry at Wikipedia. I clicked on it, but before I could start reading, Jess sucked a sharp intake of breath. "What is *that???*"

I started and looked around, expecting to find a giant spider-thing crouched in the corner and rubbing its forelegs together (*trick or treat!!!*). "What?"

"That-That book!"

Oh.

Heh.

Jess's eyes narrowed to slits and her lips screwed up in a dour pucker. "I thought you took it back."

"I forgot."

She blew a frustrated sigh. "Forgot?"

"Yes, I forgot. It happens. Now hush. I'm trying to read something." I bent over the phone and scrolled through the page. "Oh wow."

Jess hesitated a moment, torn between outrage and curiosity. "What?" she finally asked, the latter having won.

"This lady who owned the book, she's on Wikipedia."

"Wikipedia?"

"I know, right? C'mere."

She got up and came over. I scooted to the side to make room; she was kinda rigid when she sat down, and was warily eyeing the book like it might attack the moment she looked away. She risked darting her eyes to the screen, but kept the book in her line of sight; if it made one wrong move, brother, she was *gone*.

"W-What's it say?"

"Read for yourself," I said. We huddled together like two Eskimos for warmth.

The article wasn't very long or detailed (meaning Ellie Rimbaugh was important...just not *that* important) but it didn't have to be, we got the gist. Born in a log cabin south of present day Pickett's Meade in 1721, Ellie Rimbaugh was a milkmaid and all-around normal teenage girl for her time; she did the wash, swept, cooked, didn't vote, and went to bed at 7pm. One day, she was caught with a farmhand...as in "with." Y'know what I'm talking about.

Since it was 1739, doing that kind of thing before marriage was a big no-no. The townspeople were scandalized and banished her from the community; even her family disowned her. Jeez, all for getting a little nookie? I know it was the 1700s, but wow.

With nowhere else to go, she lived in a cave outside town - how she survived the harsh Virginia winters, I'll never know.

In the fall of 1744, a little boy went missing from town. Ellie, being the local hermit/witch/weirdo, was immediately suspected and arrested. After a "brief" trial (read: probably unfair), Ellie was convicted of consorting with Satan and of vanishing that kid for "darke and unholee purpuses."

You don't want to know what happened next.

It involves fire and a stake...and not the kind you eat.

But seriously, as I read Ellie Rimbaugh's fate, I could almost *feel* the fire licking my body and *taste* the woody smoke in my lungs. Here's a secret: I think burning alive would be the *worst* way to die. Just imagine the heat, your flesh beginning to bubble and blister, the clawing panic as the fire rises around you, choking the air, scalding your face, consuming you in its deadly embrace...

It literally sends a shiver down my spine.

Jess and I looked at each other; from her ashy face and flaring nostrils, she was just as shaken as I was. "Okay," Jess held up her forefingers, "I am officially creeped out. Get this book away from me."

I couldn't blame her for that sentiment; however, it's still just a book. "I doubt this is even hers," I said. "It's probably a reproduction or something. Or a hoax. Look at this thing and tell me it's five hundred years old."

Jerking her head away, Jess jumped to her feet. "I'm not looking at that thing. Get it away. It's yuck."

I looked at it and frowned. Hoax or not, Ellie Rimbaugh certainly lived and was said to have powers, and her name was right there in faded ink.

Which made the tome muy spookyoso.

And what's my middle name?

Even so, a voice in the back of my head told me Jess was right. In all honesty, she has a far better head on her shoulders than me, and I should really, really listen to her.

I opened my mouth, but a muffled honking cut me off.

Ooooh, Tim's here.

I got to my feet and tucked the book under my arm. "C'mon, Jess, our gentlemen callers have arrived."

"But -"

But I was already gone. It was Halloween night, my bf was here, and we were gonna party hardy, everything else was *whoosh* right out the window.

In the living room, Dad sat in his recliner with his feet up and a can of Coke between his legs and Mom perched at the edge of the couch, arms folded over her chest. On TV, the nightly news played: Donald Trump waved his middle finger at the press while Mike Pence facepalmed. Dad sniffed, pointed the remote at the screen, and changed it to AMC, where *Night of the Living Dead* was just starting.

"They're coming to get you, Jess," I intoned.

The horn honked again, forestalling her reply.

"Really?" Mom asked testily. "They're not going to come to the door?"

"They know better than that," Dad said.

Mom blew a raspberry. "You won't do anything."

Dad lifted his brow. "I can go get my gun if you want."

Before Mom could reply, I hooked my thumb at the door. "Okay, we're gonna head out."

"Have fun," Dad called.

"Be careful," Mom said. She jabbed a stern finger at me and lowered her brows, which meant whatever she was going to say next...she meant it. "No later than ten."

"Alright."

"Jess," Mom added, "keep her in line."

Pfft. Jess? The boss of *me*? As freaking if.

Outside, cool purple twilight inched toward night and a heatless wind slipped through the trees. Gangs of kids in costumes of every kind - oooh, nice Hulk - roamed up and down the sidewalks with empty sacks. There was a princess, a ghost, a little Dracula, and even someone in a full Iron Man suit. Lookin' good, Stark.

Tim's car, a battered blue Oldsmobile Cutlass he bought on the cheap from his grandma sat at the curb, its one good headlight dim and sickly. I pick on him *mercilessly* about that car, but while I can get him everywhere else, I can't get him there...'cause at least he *has* a ride. The harsh orange glare of a streetlamp highlighted the many dings and rust spots flecking the paint job and backlit the interior, reducing Tim and Mark to silhouettes, Tim behind the wheel and Mark in the passenger seat, ramrod straight like he had a stick up his butt. Swinging the book back and forth like a happy elf with her lunch pail, I brushed past Jess and went down the walkway. "Alexes first," I tossed over my shoulder.

I shifted the book to my left hand and opened the back door, then slid in. The smell of McDonald's grabbed me by the front of my dress and shoved its tongue down my throat (what, no dinner first?) and I retched a little. "This car reeks," I moaned.

Tim sighed. "I sprayed Febreeze before I came over."

Jess climbed in beside me and pulled the door closed behind her. "Hey," she said to Mark.

"Hey," he said without turning. "You look nice."

"You haven't even seen me," she said, flattered.

"I don't need to. You always look nice."

She giggled.

Ooooh, good one, Mark.

Tim put the car in drive and pulled away from the curb.

I waited a few seconds, then cleared my throat. He glanced questioningly in the rearview mirror. "Aren't you gonna compliment me?" I asked.

"You look nice."

I sighed.

"What?"

"It's not the same when I have to *tell* you."

"Sorry."

Boys. You can't live with them; you can't dunk their heads in water then dispose of their wet, lifeless corpses in the street as a warning to the others.

"Where's your costume?" I asked.

"I'm wearing it."

A bar of light flicked across the car; Tim wore a pair of dark overalls. "Your work clothes?"

"No."

We pulled to a red light, and he pulled a mask over his face, then turned.

"Oh, Michael Myers," I said, like greeting an old friend. "What about you, Marky-Mark? What are you dressed up as?"

He reached into the breast pocket of his Izod, yanked something out, and shoved it into his mouth. He turned and gave me a big, fangy smile.

"Vampire," I nodded, "a classic." I stole a sidelong glance at Jess and an evil smile carved across my face. Should I say it? No, it was *waaaay* too risqué. Then again, I *do* enjoy pushing the envelope. "Maybe you can use those on Jessy later."

Jess shot me daggers (ow) and though I couldn't be sure on account of the darkness, I think her face turned fire truck red.

"I'd rather not," Mark said, missing my meaning entirely. "I don't *really* drink blood."

"You don't say." My hand brushed something and I looked down at the seat. The book, face as frozen in torment as ever. "So, the other day at the library, I found *this*." I held it up, and Tim and Mark both glanced at it. I couldn't see Jess but I could *feel* her paling.

I opened the cover and flipped a few pages. "It's a spellbook. It belonged to a real live witch."

"Yeah?" Tim asked, mildly interested.

"Yeah, I looked her up on Wikipedia."

He turned to look at me, eyebrows raised. "Wikipedia? You know she's legit if she's on Wikipedia."

"Exactly."

I told him and Mark everything, starting with finding the book in the storeroom and ending with what I dug up about Ellie Rimbaugh. "Wait," Tim said, "that's thing's bound in human flesh?"

"..."

"Alex."

Firm.

Demanding.

"N-No." I doubted it really was, but I honestly couldn't be sure. Like I said earlier, that book was *not* 500 years old and if it was really wrapped in skin, said skin would have decayed and rotted long ago.

I said as much, and he spared me a quick, uneasy glance. "Don't spag out. It's not really skin."

"It's creepy, whatever it is," Jess shuddered.

"You're *all* lightweights."

Two miles later, we turned onto Pine Street...

...and Tim hit the brake. He, Jess, and Mark were wearing their seatbelts. I was not, and the force of the stop flung me into the back of Tim's seat. "Ow!" I cried more in surprise than pain. "Why did you - ?"

Then I saw it. The Brenners' was ahead on the right, a virtual palace with dormers, marble columns, French doors, and decorations in the yard. A fleet of cop cars, blue lights streaking the night, sat at the curb, and people in costumes knelt and sat on the front lawn, some in handcuffs and others looking ashamed. A couple cops in black stood over them, one looking at a clipboard and another shoving someone into the back of a car. The perp was tall, thin, and balding with glasses. I was pretty sure it was Alton Brenner.

Uh...what's going on?

"Oh, my God," Jess breathed, horrified.

Tim sighed and hung his head, and Mark silently counted. "Ten cops."

Another squad car appeared and parked, and two more got out. "Twelve cops."

Throwing the car in reverse, Tim backed up, and my heart clutched. "B-But the party."

"Party's canceled," he said bitterly.

Great.

I blew a puff of air and slumped back against my seat. My lip may or may not have stuck sullenly out. I don't know. I was certainly upset enough. "I knew it," Jess said. "I knew something would go wrong; I *knew* there'd be illegal activity – I knew it, I knew it, I knew it." She shuddered and hugged herself like she was cold. "Thank *God* it happened before we got there."

Well, what could I say? Jess was right. I told her this party was on the level and it wasn't, which made me look really bad.

Even worse, though...no party! No bobbing for apples, no seasonal music, no dancing, no cake walks, no pin the tail on the donkey, no punch, no snacks, no costumes, nothing.

Halloween was officially ruined.

"What now?" Tim asked and looked at me in the mirror.

My stomach rumbled. "Well, first, I'm hungry, then…" I trailed off. What? It was Halloween and on Halloween you do Halloweeny things. In Pickett's Meade, you had the Brenners' party or trick-or-treating, and that was pretty much it. Except for the haunted house at the volunteer fire department, but that stank: It was the same set up and same cheap jump scares every year. Yawn. And as much as I like free candy, I'm just a little too old for trick-or-treating...just ask the *bigots* in this town. *Durr, you're fifteen, durr, you're too old, durr stop shoving little kids out of the way to be first durr.*

All the way to Burger King I wracked my brain for something fun and festive we could do. We could throw eggs and soap windows, but for one thing, it was too early for that, everyone was still awake, and for two, I might be a lot of things, but I am *not* a hoodlum. Tim crept to the order window, grabbed some Whoppers, fries and Cokes, then pulled to the exit. Clock's ticking, Alex.

Tight, gripping claustrophobia closed around my chest, and the prospect of missing Halloween, my favorite holiday, made me want to hyperventilate, Jessy style.

"We could go to the Jesusween party at the Methodist church," Mark offered.

UGH. No. I want Halloween, not some evangelical knock off - no offense to my Christian friends. Jesus is a fine boy and all, but his parties aren't my cup of Joe. Place was probably a -

A metaphorical light bulb appeared over my head. "The cemetery!"

Jess's face fell.

"The cemetery?" Tim asked incredulously.

"Why the cemetery?" Mark put in.

Pfft. Why the cemetery? What a normie. "It's quiet, it's dark...and it is *spooky*. Perfect for a little Halloween revelry."

"I-I don't wanna go to the cemetery," Jessy stammered.

Sigh. Of course not. Jess just *has* to be the wet blanket of the group.

"I dunno," Tim said and turned right. In the direction of the cemetery. "That sounds kind of boring."

"We can tell scary stories," I said, "and hang out. Come on, it'll be fun."

The way I saw it, hanging out among the tombstones and telling scary stories was all we had. It wasn't optimal, but, you know, we could turn it into a good time.

Tim hummed thoughtfully.

"I really don't want to do this," Jess said.

"Why? Scared of the living dead?"

"No! It's just..." she searched for a convincing excuse, because she was *totally* afraid of the living dead. "It's disrespectful."

"No it's not. It's not like we're gonna have a Satanic orgy or desecrate graves or anything; we're just gonna chill."

Jess pursed her lips. "We're going to do this, aren't we?"

Ten minutes later, we pulled up to the main gate of Westvale Cemetery, a vast, flat, tabletop parcel of land separating the river from Westvale Drive and enclosed by a wrought iron fence. Standing in front of the archway leading in, you could look down Main Street and see the sparse lights of downtown. A few houses with big yards salted Westvale and the lamps were spaced far apart, leaving the night to hold court. Overhead, stars splashed the dark sky like diamond chips on black velvet, and a crisp breeze stirred the trees. Tim parked at the curb and cut the engine. Shadows filled the car, and seeing Jess's face five inches from my own was nigh on impossible.

"Just for the record," she said and chopped the air for emphasis, "I do *not* like this."

I opened my door and got out. "Don't be a spoil sport."

Tim and Mark followed, and Jess hesitated for a moment, then reluctantly brought up the rear. We stood next to the car and looked up at the gate: WESTVALE read the letters over the arch. A cold gust of wind swept from the south, and Jess hugged herself. "I didn't think I'd need my jacket." The glare she gave me made her comment feel like an accusation.

Mark put his arm around her shoulders, and she gratefully leaned into him like a warmth-sucking vampire. "There's a blanket in the trunk," Tim said and went around the back, opened the trunk, then came back with a heavy wool comforter that he handed her before turning to me. "How are we going to get in there?" A thick chain was threaded through the bars and padlocked in place. Huh. That *might* present a problem. I walked over, bent, and studied it closely.

It looked formidable.

"I dunno, but it's not looking good, guys." I reached out and touched it.

Two things happened at once. One, shock went up my left arm, traveled through my chest like an electric gas bubble, and went down my right arm; two, the padlock popped open and fell to the ground.

"Y'ouch!" I ripped my hand back, even though it didn't hurt...it just kind of tingled.

"What?" Tim asked worriedly.

I looked at my fingertips and flexed them slowly.

They looked and felt normal.

"That lock shocked me." I kicked it aside. "Must be corroded or something."

I stripped the chain out with a clang and dropped it on the ground; it landed with a hollow thump and kicked up a little poof of dust.

"Uhh...maybe we shouldn't," Jess said. "This is technically breaking and entering."

"No it's not." I opened the gate and the rusted hinges shrieked like an eerie banshee cry, making me wince.

Like I said, Jess has a good head on her shoulders, perhaps I should listen to her.

Then again: Halloween.

That decided me. "C'mon guys, follow me to fun."

A gravel road bisected the grounds, a narrow sliver to the left and a broad plain broken by trees and headstones on the right. Westvale had been Picketts Meade's primary burying place - in one form or another - since the 1850s, and as such, it was *kind* of packed. The slabs, crypts, vaults, and gravestones were crammed together. Closer to the entrance, the graves were newer, but the farther back you went, the older they got: Crooked, slanted, covered in slime, moss, and grit, the writing on their faces had largely been worn by years and the elements. The ground in front of a few was sunken and uneven; it took me a minute to realize that was probably because the coffins below had collapsed.

Creepy.

An owl hooted from a high branch, and Jess let out a squeaky *eep* and then moaned. "Let's go."

"But we just got here," I said.

"I wanna go home." It came in a fearful rush that made her sound like a little girl in a scary place. She hugged herself tightly, and Mark pulled her close with a whispered word of encouragement I didn't catch. Tim moseyed along with his hands in his pockets, looking curiously around like he'd never seen a cemetery before. The moon crested over the rim of the earth, and a shaft of silvery light fell on an inexplicable wide spot between two rows, set just far enough from the surrounding stones to make it perfect for chilling without being on top of the dead. The grass was thick, dry, and soft.

That sounded dirty.

Going over, I dropped to my butt and crossed my legs. I patted the ground next to me. "C'mon, Jess, I'll protect you from the living dead."

Jess sputtered. "D-Don't talk about them."

"Why not? I asked. "Scared?" Throwing my head back, I deepened my voice. "They're not coming to get you, Jess. Look, there goes one of them now...in the opposite direction."

Poor Jess shook like a leaf. "D-Don't say that." She got stiffly to her knees then sat, and cowered against Mark for comfort.

Tim sank to his butt beside me and drew his knees to his chest. The moon soared into the sky like a vampire waking from infernal slumber, and its cold light bathed the cemetery. It was so bright I could see halfway across the field. Something moved, and a thrill went up my leg like my name was Chris Matthews.

That means max spookiness has been achieved. Give yourself a pat on the back, Alex.

I went to do that, but there was something in my left hand.

Something flesh-ish.

And booky.

Huh. Have I really been carrying this thing the whole time? I tried to remember picking it up, holding it on the walk over, but couldn't.

Okay, *now* max spookiness has been achieved.

From Tim's exasperated sigh, he noticed the book. "Did you really have to bring that?"

"It was in my hand. I totally forgot about it." I set it in the grass in front of me, slapped my hands on my knees, and looked around at my squad: Jess, pale and shaking; Mark looking around (fascinating tree); and Tim sneering at the book like it burned his crops and salted the earth so nothing would ever grow again. "You act like it's the worst thing ever."

Tim favored me with a toxic sidelong glance. "Alex...it's covered in human skin."

66

Oh, *this* again? As the President might say: You, sir, are fake news. "It's not really human skin. It's not – here; feel." I realized even as those words left my mouth that the cover *did* feel like skin - warm, living skin - and that Tim feeling it *probably* wouldn't help my case.

Thankfully, he politely declined. "Get that shit away from me."

"I wanna hold it," Mark said.

Aha, Mark, my man.

"Ew, God, don't touch it," Jess said. "Alex, please get rid of that book."

The beseeching hilt in her voice was raw and abject. "I will tomorrow, okay? But...come on, it's Halloween, and Sheriff Brackett says: Everyone's entitled to one good scare. You don't wanna let Sheriff Brackett down. Do you?"

"I don't even know who that is," Jess snapped. Her patience was wearing thin, and one good prod would rip it to shreds...like 1-ply toilet paper.

"He's the -"

Jess threw her head back. "I don't care. I don't like being scared. And I don't like that book."

"Yeah, I'm not into it either," Tim concurred.

Alright, real talk: I was starting to get offended. Don't ask me why, I know it doesn't make sense, but their babified bellyaching irked me. Maybe I was mad over the party being ruined, maybe I was taking it personally when I shouldn't have, or maybe...maybe the book was even then exerting some kind of sick pall over me.

Or maybe it was a combination of those things.

Or maybe it was none of them.

Whatever it may or may not have been, my face flushed hotly and my chest roiled. Bunch of bellyaching babies. If they think this book was creepy now, just you wait, buddy.

I struggled to my feet and stood over them like an ax-wielding psycho. "I tried to reason with you, but noooo." I opened the cover. "My name is Alex Warner, and I'm a real live witch now. This book is *mine* and I'm going to curse *all* of you with it."

Tim rolled his eyes; Mark stared blankly; and Jess clenched her jaw.

I opened the cover, and a gust of wind caught the pages. When they fluttered back into place, I read the text. Oooh, perfect. "Latin," I said nastily, "the language of *Satan.*" I threw up a one-handed air quote.

"Knock it off, Alex," Jess said firmly.

"It's too late for that, Jessica. You mocked me and now you will pay...by becoming a frog and thinking about what you've done."

Squinting to see in the dim moonlight, I started to read.

"Populo mortui resurgunt. Egressus est de terra."

The words felt strange and clunky on my lips, and I stumbled in a few places as I tried to sound them out.

"Voco vos ad vigilaveris."

A sudden wind gusted through the cemetery, stirring my hair.

"Redire ad hoc terra."

The words came easier, as though I *wasn't* speaking Latin for the first time ever. The book seemed to pulse in my hands like a beating heart and energy surged through my veins. Another gust, this one stronger; my dress and hair rippled around me, and the edge of the page blew back and forth. My heart slammed against my ribs and I tried to stop, but some outside force pulled me through the rite.

"Venit ex monumentis. Excitare. Finem somno et excitare."

My voice echoed in my head, and I realized I was numb. Fear flooded my chest...but the otherworldly exhilaration was stronger. I felt big, powerful, and maybe, I'm ashamed to say, a little sexually excited.

Jess screamed, and for the first time ever, Mark's features arranged in the shape of human emotion.

He looked scared.

"Alex!" Tim cried, barely audible over the shrieking wind. Trees swayed, leaves pelted my back and stuck in my hair. "Stop!"

I'm trying!!!

Instead, more Latin spilled from my mouth. *"Surgere nunc. Ego obsecramus te. Nocte pertinet ad te."*

Jess buried her face in Mark's chest; Tim held his arm up to shield himself from the wind, and Mark turned his head. A long, crashing peal of thunder rent the night, and lightning cracked the sky. A tremor ran through the ground and my mind screamed at me to stop, for the love of God, STOP IT!!!

My lips moved on their own, my mouth spoke but not my voice. This voice was deeper, darker, and coming out, it felt almost like it was being *dragged*, a fish at the end of a hook. *"Veni et accipe nocte! Excitare! Excitare!"*

Like throwing a switch, it stopped. The thunder rumbled to silence, the lightning faded, and the wind died down. The book was red hot and shaking from side to side like a small, vicious animal, and with a cry, part pain and part alarm, I threw it down and fell back a step; my feet tangled in the hem of my dress and I landed on my butt so hard the air drove from my lungs.

Jess cowered into Mark, terrified whimpers rising from her hitching chest, and Tim lay curled in the grass like a baby in the womb. I'm pretty sure he would have been crying for mommy if his vocal cords weren't frozen.

Me? I sat there in shock, cast, for once, into total silence. I know I can be kind of silly and maybe even a little annoying, but right then and there, all of that dried up.

What the hell just happened?

I darted my eyes to the book.

Still.

Dark.

But somehow...I could feel its presence...as though it weren't an inanimate object but a person.

"What the hell, Alex?" Tim groaned shakily.

"T-That wasn't me!"

"Yes it was," Mark said.

"Honest! I -"

Something brushed my hand and I yanked it away with a gasp. I turned my head, but didn't see anything.

Whew.

On edge. Heh. "It was the book."

"I told you it was yuck," Jess said.

I know, God, I know, you were so right, Jess, I'm sorry.

Before I could say that - or anything else - a flicker of movement caught my attention. I turned again just as a clump of earth moved aside and a gray, withered hand emerged. My heart dropped into my stomach and my mouth fell open. Long, bony fingers quested across the grass like the world's most petrifying spider, and I stared at them in skull-cracking horror. Yellowed bone showed through hanging tatters of flesh, and a bug scuttled over one knotted knuckle.

Zombie.

The world around me dimmed and my mind came *this* close to breaking.

No.

T-That's not possible.

Zombies aren't real.

ZOMBIES AREN'T REAL!!!

The hand lifted higher, turning slightly left to right as if tasting the cool night air. *Hey, haven't felt* this *in a while.*

"Holy shit!"

Tim jumped up like a startled cat and nearly fell over Jess and Mark. An arm was reaching out of the ground where he had just been lying, and the hand was opening and closing spasmodically as if to say, *I know you're there, buster, c'mere.*

My paralysis broke, and with a throat rending screech, I rocketed to my feet and spun around.

As soon as my brain registered what my eyes were seeing, I really, really, *really* wished I hadn't turned around.

71

They were *everywhere*. Arms and torsos struggled from the earth; dark figures shambled between the rows; nearby, a woman looking like something from *They Live* pulled herself out of her grave, her ratty burial dress clinging to her emaciated form. Farther away, a man in a dusty suit used a headstone to draw himself to a standing position. Most of the flesh had rotted away from his skull, and one milky-white eye stared out from a yawning socket with malevolent life. Our gazes met, and the look of hungry excitement that flickered across his visage stopped my heart in its tracks.

"Oh my God!" Jess wailed. She rocked on her butt, pitched forward, hit the ground face first, and flailed like a no-limb woman in an ass-kicking contest. Mark pulled her to her feet, and they both staggered. Tim stared down at the ghoul before him with wide-eyed shock. It had worked itself free to the waist, and snatched at him with a low, doggish growl.

Others were coming, all skeletal faces, sparse hair, gaping eye sockets, squirming maggots, teeth, lipless smiles; their voices came together in a hellish din of moaning, and the sound alone was enough to shove me back. Jess was sobbing and Mark looked quickly around for a weapon, but there was nothing. I realized I was hyperventilating and tried to calm myself, but a hand grabbed my ankle, and I let loose a terrified howl instead.

A skeleton lay prone in front of me, its frame stripped of skin, blood, muscle, and everything else that makes a person. It lifted its head, and impossibly, it had eyes: Blue, bloodshot, and moist with intelligence. My body froze and hysteria burst inside my head like a dying heart.

Suddenly, Tim was beside me, his foot falling in a deadly arc; it hit the skull, and with a wet, sickening snap, it came off and rolled away. "Motherfucker," it called.

God, they can talk???

"Come on!" Tim wrenched me back and we fell in beside Mark and Jess, a tiny, huddled group facing a thousand enemies in various states of decay. They lurched, crawled, hobbled, one even used a branch as a rudimentary cane. They hissed, spat, and mewled like animals.

Even though I was seeing it, I couldn't believe it.

Jess hugged herself and bent at the waist, crying harder now. Mark took her by the arm and slowly led her away, as if afraid to make any sudden moves. Something grabbed me, and I screamed, but it was only Tim. "Come on!"

I turned to run, but a zombie was there, and I went stiff. My height, maybe an inch shorter, it had been a man in life. Rags hung from its arms in shreds and its slime-coated ribcage stuck out from bluish skin. Tufts of wispy white hair clung to its skull and its empty eye sockets festered with worms. Tim put his arm protectively around me but made no move to fight the thing. So much for bravery, huh?

The thing leaned over, and, as one, Tim and I leaned back.

Sniffing the air, the zombie made an obscene *ummmmm* sound. "Your brain smells spicy, like a fajita."

Wait, what did he say? "Okay, wow, that was really racist."

Its maggot bitten tongue swiped over what passed for its upper lip. "I-I don't think he cares about being politically correct," Tim said through his teeth.

Jess screamed, and she and Mark started to run. Tim grabbed my hand, pulled me away from the zombie, and together, we ran too. Ghouls stumbled after us, arms raised and teeth gnashing, some so close I could feel their fingertips grazing my arm, which only made me run faster.

Ahead, Jess and Mark made it through the gate. A few zombies staggered into our way, but we swung wide. A hot stitch flared in my side and fire filled my lungs, but I ignored it. My survival instincts were in full gear and absolutely nothing else mattered.

I got through the gate first, and Tim a split second later. Jess and Mark ran down the middle of Main toward town, their feet flying over the pavement. The hellish sounds of a tortured multitude rose behind us. "Hey, dumbasses, get in the car!" I yelled.

Someone snagged my dress and whipped me around. A mountain of cold, decomposing flesh clad in a white tall T. I looked up, and a dead face sneered down at me.

Three years is a long time, but the creature before me kept remarkably well.

So well that I recognized him instantly.

Cornrows, grill.

Wilko the White Rapper.

And he was *much* taller in person.

"What the fuck is y'all doin' in my cemetery?" he demanded.

The zombies were almost at the gate, a wall of dark faces and even darker desire.

"Hey," Tim started, but Wilko cut him off.

"Nigga, shut yo ass up. I ain't talkin to you. I'm talkin' to lil' miss Mexi-bitch."

Tim took a threatening step forward, and in a flash, Wilko pushed me away and grabbed him around the throat with both hands Wayne Brady style. Tim's eyes bulged and his lips smooshed together. Wilko held him off the ground, and his feet kicked back and forth. "What, nigga?" Wilko asked and shook him like a crocodile with its prey. "What, nigga?"

The vanguard reached the gate and the living dead began to spill out into the night, the ones at the head of the pack mere feet away. I turned to Wilko, terror clawing my heart. If I didn't do something, Tim was -

It hit me, and summoning all my strength, I threw a punch.

At Wilko's balls.

His eye widened and his grip on Tim released. He dropped to one knee and shuddered in agony. "Bitch," he panted, "you done fucked up now."

When he looked up, though, we were already gone.

CHAPTER FOUR

At the same time all of *that* was going down, my boy Langston was stuck at work. Alone. With Pat. Pfft, I'd *rather* have zombies.

That night, three people (counting Pat) were supposed to work in addition to Langston, but two of them - Kyle and Amber - called out.

You'd think it was to party or go trick-or-treating, but nope.

They had mono.

AKA: The Kissing Disease.

We all know what *that* means.

Their tongues were in each other's mouths.

Anyway, Langston was trapped at Pissy's with Pat and probably hating every minute of it. See, Pat's like a socialist; he spreads the wealth around, the "wealth" in this case being his B.S. Since Amber and Kyle were out, that meant he heaped all of it on Langston. He bitched because the bathrooms weren't clean (even though they were), he ordered Langston to scrub the fryers just for the sake of issuing an order, he even made Langston get on a wobbly chair and dust the overhead lights (whoooa, be careful!). All the while, Pat stood there with a smug expression on his greasy little mug. He just *loved* telling people what to do.

Makes sense, I guess; he's completely powerless in every other aspect of his life, so when he gets to work, where he has a modicum of control, it goes *straight* to his head.

Langston bore all of this with a stoicism you just can't help but respect. He mopped and re-mopped the bathrooms, made the fryers *sparkle*, took out the quarter-full trash, swept cigarette butts out of the parking lot, dusted the lights, cleaned the tables, made pizzas, *and* was always right there at the register when someone needed him. He didn't sweat, he didn't roll his eyes; his face remained sleepy, eyes drooping, expressionless expression (is that an oxymoron?). All that mattered to him was making enough money to track down Quentin Tarantino and avenge Bruce Lee. If he had to put up with Pat, so be it.

Just past eight, Pat locked himself in the office to do "filing" but I'd bet money he was really drawing a nine-year-old boy doing his seventeen-year-old sister. Or maybe he was using the PC to throw his weight around that fandom he's in. Either way, Langston was finally alone. He stood behind the counter, shoulders slumped, and waited for someone to come in.

Outside, four kids tore past in the street, screaming bloody murder, and Langston watched with dull apathy. I like to think he recognized me and thought *Hey, there's Alex...she looks cool even when she's running for her life*, but, let's be honest, folks, he most likely didn't.

Moments after we passed, a large, sloppy group of people in dirty burial suits and dresses filled the street. Many walked at a gait, but some of the fresher ones moved a little quicker. Moaning, arms outstretched, feet dragging behind them, they looked like either homeless people escaped from L.A., or the most dedicated bunch of *Thriller* cosplayers this side of the eighties. Aw, great, Langston thought, the Brenners' party let out early.

On the bright side, maybe they'll want some pizza.

Two men split from the pack and came to the door. Their coats and pants were muddy and ripped, just like their flesh, and one had a gaping hole in his left cheek. Nice makeup.

One opened the door and they shuffled in, their steps uncertain, shoes scraping the tiles and leaving clumps of dirt in their wake.

Fabulous, Langston thought, just incredible. Wanna screw up the john, too?

They came up to the counter...

...and studied the menu overhead.

One of them smacked his lips together and looked at Langston. His voice was deep and raspy, almost like he'd been eating dirt for the past sixty years. "Can I get a large anchovy and brain pizza, please?"

Langston arched his brow. "Brain?"

The zombie smiled nervously. *I was hoping you wouldn't notice my strange request*, it seemed to say.

"We don't have brains here," Langston said. "If we did, we'd work somewhere else."

The zombie sagged disappointedly. "Alright, just anchovies."

Langston looked at the other one: It squinted at the menu, then held its hand to its forehead to cut out the glare of the lights. "Your wings, do they come in people flavor?"

"No, they do not," Langston said, becoming irritated. "This is a normal pizza parlor. If you want something like that, you're gonna have to go to Dahmer's House of Cannibalism down the street."

The zombies both perked up. "Can you give us directions?"

Sigh.

Langston opened his mouth to explain he was joking, but the door crashed open and another zombie lurched in, this one so badly decomposed that its skull was exposed. A web crisscrossed one eye socket and the spider that made it scurried into its mouth as it approached the counter. It shoved the other two out of its way, leaned over, and grabbed the front of Langston's shirt, pulling him close. "*Brains*!"

In his usual flat-toned voice, Langston said, "Sir, can you get your hands off of me?"

The first two zombies looked from Skull Face to Langston and back again like Old West townspeople warily watching a pair of dueling gunslingers.

"*Brains!*" Skull Face repeated. Its fetid breath raped Langston's nose, and the chill of its touch sank into his bones.

"Sir, now I'm telling you. Next time I won't be nice about it. Get your hands off of me."

Skull Face leaned closer. Now its noseless nasal cavity was inches from Langston's lips. "What are *you* gonna do, fat boy?"

Langston froze.

Apparently, when he was in school, kids used to tease Langston about his weight. A lot. In seventh grade, he weighed close to 210 and everyone made fun of him for it. They called him Tubby, Lard-ass, Fatso, and a bunch of other really hurtful names. They made him sit by himself at lunch and no one ever played with him at recess or had so much as a kind word to say. A girl he liked found out about his crush on her, and told him to his face that she'd never date "a tub of lard like you." He was isolated, sad, and hated himself.

Then he found Bruce Lee movies, and watching Bruce fly around the screen beating up bad guys made life a little more manageable. Langston took up kung-fu and lost most of the junk in his trunk, though some still stuck.

Where was I? Oh, yeah, anyway, calling him fat was the exact *wrong* thing to do. All those bad memories, all that hatred - of his bullies *and* himself - all those friendless days in middle school and dateless nights in high school, all the taunts, jeers, name calling...all of that crap came back to him in a rush.

And he fucking *flipped.*

First, bright red crept across his face, then his lips peeled back from his teeth. He started to shake like a powder keg getting ready to blow, and boiling rage shot up from his stomach like Old Faithful, only hotter.

Fast as quicksilver, he grabbed the zombie's hand and twisted, breaking it off from the wrist with a dry crunch. Screaming, he brought his arm up and threw out his elbow, hitting Skull Face across the chin. The zombie's head whipped to one side and it stumbled back.

All of Langston's repressed feelings - toward Pat, Quentin Tarantino, his bullies, that rude cop who pulled him over six months ago, his I'll-fix-it-later slumlord - consumed him like a nuclear death cloud, and a switch flipped in his brain. Langston went away.

And Kung-Fu Psycho took his place.

He ripped his shirt off Hulk Hogan style and jumped onto the counter, then ducked and hit a sick spinning kick that smashed one of the zombies in the face. He jumped down on bent knees, and Skull Face rushed him. Langston threw a quick jab that shattered ribs, then followed it up with a sharp left. Skull Face fell back, shook his head, and came again, seething with undead fury. Langston jumped and did some kind of scissor kick move, and Skull Face's head flew off. Its body stayed standing, though, and Langston kicked it again. This time, it toppled over, hit the floor, and broke into a thousand pieces.

Panting, Langston stood over his foe, then, remembering the others, he spun and held his open hands up to his face, ready to chop the first thing he saw. One of the zombies fell on him, and Langston sidestepped, hitting it across the back. It turned, and Langston danced from one foot to the other, fists up, face drenched in sweat. The zombie faked a step, then launched at Langston.

"Waaaaah HI-YAH!"

Langston's fist crashed into the zombie's nose, broke through its weakened facial structure, and sank deep into its slime-filled brain cavity. The ghoul lost its fight and went limp.

Dead – for good.

Ripping his hand out like Excalibur from the fabled stone, Langston turned on the third zombie.

The zombie looked him up and down...then backed slowly to the door, hands up. "Hey, man, I don't want any trouble." It bumped into the door, felt behind it for the handle, and slipped out into the night. Langston watched it hurry away. There were more in the street, all making their way west.

Like a rabid dog with the taste of blood in its mouth, Langston couldn't stop...wouldn't stop.

Not until his wrath had been spent.

Going around the end of the counter, he reached into a drawer and pulled something reverently out. A white headband with a big red dot on the front.

The Japanese Rising Sun.

He stretched it taut, threaded it around his brow, and tied it just as the office door opened and Pat swaggered, all five-foot-four inches of him. "What the hell was that noise? Were you watching Bruce Lee movies on your phone again?" He noticed Langston's bare chest and sputtered. "Put your shirt back on! What are you doing?"

Pat was the type of man who just didn't know when to quit. He got closer and closer to Langston, griping the entire way. Langston's eyes narrowed, and when Pat was in striking distance, he curled his fingertips against his palm and shot out his arm. The heel took Pat in the temple, and the fat, pervy fandom hack dropped like a sack of dirty diapers, knocked unconscious.

Langston glowered down at him...then went off to find more ass to kick.

I stumbled, started to fall, and threw my arms around a stop sign. Tim stopped next to me, clasped his hands to his knees, and bent over, back rising and falling with the seething tide of his exhalations. Mark leaned against a tree, and Jess slumped her shoulders.

We were on a residential street corner surrounded by lower middle class houses. Lights burned in windows and over front doors, but the sidewalks were empty. I don't recall passing anyone on the way, but I was *kind* of preoccupied.

"Where are we?" Tim panted.

After we got away from Wilko, we booked it, our only thought to put as much distance between us and the ravenous horde as possible. I looked around for a guidepost, but nothing was familiar. Not the yards, not the ranch houses presiding over them, not the street signs. Where were we? Oh, God, where were we?

Cool night wind rustled the trees and brought the sound of distant moaning to my ears.

Come on, come on, I've been all over this dumb town; I *know* this place, I just have to think, think—freaking think! Let's see, let's see, let's see: I remember going through downtown, so we have to be on the west side. Home is there too.

Must have come this way on instinct. I looked around again, turning in a slow, stricken circle.

Then I saw it.

A mailbox shaped like a bass.

I knew that mailbox. I passed it every day on the way to school. Jess called it tacky, but I thought it was neat.

"This way," I said.

No sooner had I spoken, six zombies emerged from the dark behind us. My breath caught and my heart dropped to my feet.

One spotted me and pointed. "There they are!"

Jess glanced over her shoulder and screamed.

"Come on!" I snatched Jess by the wrist and started running.

"Get 'em!" the zombie yelled.

A strangled sob exploded from Jess's throat, and she pumped her arms and legs to match my pace. Tim and Mark were behind me...I think. I won't lie, my only thought was for myself and Jess. That sounds selfish, but *you* try getting chased by the undead.

Our street appeared to the right. My hold on Jess's hand broke, and she went to her knees. I stopped, but Mark and Tim were already scooping her up. The zombies were twenty feet back, maybe thirty, and gaining fast. Someone whimpered, and I realized it was me.

The house sits on the left at the end of the block. The porch light was on, a beacon in the night, calling, beckoning, promising safety. I pushed myself harder, feet flying over the pavement, breath coming in hot gasps, blood crashing against my temples. I veered across the yard, reached the bottom of the steps, slid on the walkway, and fell. I sprang to my feet, trampled up the stairs, and threw myself at the door where I stopped and looked back. Tim and Mark flanked Jess, each with an arm around her shoulders. She limped heavily, hissing with every step. The zombies were fifteen feet back, now ten. My heart thudded, my stomach clinched.

Snatching the knob, I twisted and fell against the door, wrenching it open. Mom sat on the couch and Dad in his chair, her watching TV and him reading the paper. They both startled and looked up.

Tim and Mark got Jess in, and I slammed the door behind them. Jess was crying, Tim and Mark panting.

"What the hell?" Dad demanded.

Jess collapsed to the floor and gave in to her tears, and Mark dropped to one knee.

"What?" Dad asked with an edge of worry in his voice. Mom was already rushing to Jess's side and kneeling.

Tim went to the front window and peeked through the blinds like a paranoid crackhead, and I fumbled for my phone, then cussed when I didn't find it; I must have dropped it somewhere. I said something, but it came out as an incoherent babble.

Mom stroked Jess's back and shushed her, and Dad got up.

"They're out there," Tim said and backed away from the window.

"We gotta call the cops and board up the doors and windows," I said in a rush.

Dad looked from one of us to the other like we were crazy. "Alright," he said in a commanding tone - his Dad voice. "What the hell is going on here?"

"Zombies," me and Tim said in unison.

Mom's brow creased disbelievingly, and Dad's eyes creaked to mistrustful slits. He looked like I just told him something completely insane. "Zombies?"

"The undead," I said.

"Ghouls," Tim added.

"The living impaired," Mark said.

Dad looked from one of us to the other like we were nuts. "What happened, Jess?" he finally asked, because to him, she was the most trustworthy of us all.

Nice, Dad, real nice.

"Z-Zombies," she managed through her tears.

Mom deflated (*great, Jessy's crazy now too*) and Dad hung his head.

"We're telling the truth," Tim said.

"They're right outside," I confirmed. "They chased us all the way here."

Dad took a deep breath and let it out. "That's enough. There are no zombies. They're not real. They -"

"But -"

He held up a forestalling hand. "But nothing. Maybe someone played a prank on you or something, but there aren't any zombies out there."

"Yes there are," Jess hitched.

That did it.

He went to the door.

"No!" I wailed. "God, don't open the door!"

Suddenly everyone was talking at once.

"Enough!" Dad said. "I'm going to show you there aren't any damn zombies."

He unlocked the door. Jess howled, Tim winced, and I braced myself.

The door opened...

...and Dad recoiled.

Six zombies stood on the porch like a group of macabre Christmas carolers. The one in front, a short creature with a belly and the last remnants of curly brown hair on either side of a bald spot, had his hand up and balled, as though he were preparing to knock. He let it fall and cleared his throat. "Excuse me..."

He trailed off.

"Kev?" he asked uncertainly.

Dad's eyes grew to twice their normal size and his mouth fell open in surprise. The color drained from his face with an almost audible sucking sound, and for a second he gaped...then his brows lowered analytically. "D-Dale?"

Dale the zombie laughed heartily. "Well, shove a stick up my ass and call me a corndog, how ya been?"

Mom was frozen in place, breath bated. From the look of mind-bending horror in her brown eyes, I could tell that she knew Dale the zombie too.

Or had when he was alive.

"G-Good," Dad said numbly. "Y-you?"

Dale shrugged. "Remember that stomach ache I had? I shoulda gone to the doctor." He slapped his knee and grated laughter. "Anyway, look, me 'n' the boys were chasing some kids and they ran in here -"

"Yeah," Dad stammered, "my daughters."

Dale's face fell. "Ooooh."

He rubbed the back of his neck. "Well...this is awkward. I guess there's, uh, no chance of you handing them over, huh?"

"No!" Dad cried and flung the door closed.

"Alright, fellas," Dale said, voice muffled, "we're breakin' in."

Mom shook her head like a woman coming awake from a dream and gestured crazily at the door. "W-W-What was *that?*"

"Zombies." Dad's voice was low and filled with wonder.

Something slammed against the door from the outside, and it shook in its frame. Dad threw himself against it and Mom jumped to her feet. "You," Dad said and jutted his chin at Mark, "go in the master bedroom and get my gun. It's in the closet."

Mark stood and rushed off, and Mom grabbed her cell phone off the coffee table. She dialed a number then held it to her ear.

I went to the window, pushed the blinds aside, and peered out into the night. I didn't see anything, but I could hear them talking to each other. "Go break that window," Dale ordered.

"I can't do that. It's bad luck."

Dale sighed. "Really? You believe in that supernatural crap?"

"I'm literally a walking corpse – yes."

"Good point. Never mind."

Mom threw her head back. "The line's busy."

The banging grew louder as a half dozen hands beat against the door and the side of the house. Mom helped Jess up and guided her to the couch. They sat, and Mom pressed Jess's head to her chest.

Mark returned holding an assault rifle so wicked and intimidating looking that describing it too well would probably give you PTSD: black and sleek with a scope, a shoulder strap, and a curved magazine, it screamed BAN ME. Dad took it and turned to the door, which jumped and trembled in its frame. "Get back," he ordered, and Tim and I joined Mom, Mark, and Jess by the couch.

Dad unlocked the handle and fell back, and the door crashed open. Dale and the others started to come in, then froze.

"Oh, shit, he's got a gun!"

The rifle spoke, and even though I was expecting it, I jumped anyway. The reports were deafening and spent cartridges ejected from the chamber in a steady stream, hitting the floor and bouncing like brass dreidels. Rounds pelted Dale's abdomen, kicking up puffs of dust, and he fell back into the crowd, a look of pain crossing his face. Bullets struck the support beams holding up the porch roof, ripped a zombie's face half off, sent another falling back over the railing, and blew out the throat of a woman with one eye.

Screaming and falling over themselves to escape, the others scattered like roaches. Dad wedged the butt of the gun into the crook of his shoulder and followed.

Outside, a spreading army of ghouls lumbered aimlessly through the street, down the sidewalks, and across front yards. Dad missed a beat, then opened fire, hitting a skeletal man in the head. The zombies reacted by diving out of the way, ducking behind cover, or throwing themselves to the ground. "Ahhh, call the cops!" one yelled.

The rifle clicked, out of bullets, and Dad lowered it. "You don't need an AR-15, they said," he quipped. "The good guy with a gun is a myth, they said."

The mass was already coming, closing around the porch like a noose: Ten zombies, fifty, a hundred, every single one of Westvale's escapees all shambling toward him in a single, pulsing wave. He backed into the house and slammed the door. "There's too many of them." Something then seemed to occur to him, and he turned around. "What exactly happened?" How'd this start?"

Jess, Mark, and Tim all looked at me.

Feeling two inches tall, I raised my hand.

Dad's brow angled down in an angry V, and Mom glared at me like I did something wrong. "Alex, what did you do?"

"She read a cursed spellbook in the cemetery," Jess sniffed. "Then the dead came back."

Mark nodded. "That's pretty much how it happened."

"Real smart, Alex," Mom said. Her voice *dripped* with sarcasm. "Because *that* could never go wrong."

"I didn't know! I didn't think spells and zombies were actually *real*."

Something hit the door, and Dad started. "We need to cover these windows and doors." He pushed away and went over to the entertainment center. "Mark, Tim, help me with this thing. Maria, grab me a fresh clip, my .357, and a couple guns for everyone else."

While Mom went to gather Dad's arsenal, Mark took the TV off the entertainment center and set it on the coffee table, then he, Dad, and Tim moved the complex in front of the door. On the couch, Jess hugged herself and rocked back and forth like a girl in a padded room, and I stood there, lost and not knowing what to do.

The banging started again, louder and more insistent, filling my head like a death knell. Mom came back struggling with a box, and set it on the couch. "I got guns," she said.

Dad came over, bent, and rummaged around the box until he found his .357, chrome and as big as a cannon. Next, he took out a compact automatic and held it out to me. I eyed it warily. Like Spanish, shooting was a passion one of my parents tried, and failed, to pass onto me. I've never touched a gun in my life and didn't know the first thing about them - you hold it by the barrel thingie and use it as a club, right?

"Here," Dad ordered. "You got us into this mess."

That was true.

Sighing, I took the gun and turned it over in my hands. "The safety's on. Turn it off to shoot."

He held another gun out to Jess, and she looked at it as though it might bite. "Take it."

She hesitated, then took it.

When everyone had a handgun - gee, Dad has enough here to start his own right-wing militia - Dad and Tim went to the front window. Mom brought a toolbox in from the garage and Mark broke the legs off the kitchen table, then carried it into the living room. "We're gonna nail it up," Dad said. "I want -"

The window exploded in a shower of glass, and before Dad could react, a head came through, mouth wide open. It flopped against his arm, and he pulled back with a yelp. My heart stopped - if they bite you, you turn into one of them.

Dad held his arm up and studied the wound. The skin wasn't broken, only scratched.

"Yeah," the zombie said smugly. "There's plenty more where that came from, buddy."

Dad jammed the gun against its head and it went cross-eyed. "Wait! I won't do it again, I promise!"

The gun jumped, and the zombie slumped to the side. As soon as he was out of the way, a forest of arms reached through, and Dad yelled. I ran over and helped him, Tim, Mark, and Mom push the table flush with the window and hold it in place while Dad hammered it to the wall. The zombies on the other side pushed, pounded, and battered, and my arm muscles strained against the assault.

Dad stepped back, surveyed his work, and nodded. "Alright," he said, "now the rest."

Next door, Old Man Krause shuffled through his darkened living room and muttered oaths under his breath. It was late (for him) and someone was knocking on his door. Damn kids, didn't they know no porch light meant no candy?

He kicked the edge of the coffee table with his bare foot and pain detonated in the center of his sole.

Still, the incessant knocking, pounding.

Goddamn fools.

He went to the door, unlocked the knob, and ripped it open.

A group of dead people stood on his step, and he blinked in surprise, his ire suddenly gone.

The lead zombie, a man in a suit, leaned in and studied the old man's face: Wrinkles, liver spots, sallow skin, faded eyes.

Mr. Krause's heartbeat sped up and paralyzing terror gripped him.

The zombie rocked back on its heels and heaved a dejected sigh. "Never mind, guys, he's one of us."

Mumbling their disappointment, the zombies turned and filed down the stairs.

It took a minute for the zombie's words to sink in, and when they did, Mr. Krause's face screwed bitterly up.

"I don't look *that* goddamn bad," he said. "Do I?"

CHAPTER FIVE

"HI-YAH!"

Langston brought his open hand down onto the center of a zombie's head, and the reanimated corpse fell to the pavement in a quivering heap. Another came at him from behind, and he rammed his elbow back into its guts. He wrapped his arm around its neck and flung it over his shoulder. It landed atop the first, arched its back, and let out a pained groan. A third approached, and Langston jumped into the air and lashed out with his foot, nailing it in the chin. It fell to one side and lay still.

Panting, Langston admired his handiwork: A trail of broken bodies littered the street between here and Pissy's three blocks back, some of them twitching like smashed bugs and others unmoving, either dead or so damaged they might as well be.

He was currently on the western edge of downtown, brick and glass storefronts to the left and town square up ahead. Sirens rose somewhere in the distance and gunshots rang out, the echo making their position impossible to determine.

Three zombies appeared down the street staggering like drunks on their way home. They spotted Langston and started to lope toward him. Hopping from one foot to the other, Langston threw his arms behind him, ducked his head, yelled, "Naruto run!" and ran at them, feet barely touching the ground. The zombies paused, as if having second thoughts, but it was too late: Langston leapt into the air, thrust one foot out in front of him like a spear, and hit a ghoul in the head, knocking it clean off. He landed on one foot, pivoted around, and kicked another zombie in the chest; it doubled over and flew backwards, hitting a metal trash can and startling a sleeping wino into flight.

The final zombie held his fists up to his face, and he and Langston circled each other like two young bucks boutta throw down. "You wanna go, fleshbag?" the zombie asked. "Come on, I'll mess you up. I didn't beat cancer but I'll *definitely* beat you."

Langston made a move, and the zombie drew back.

"Bring it," Langston said.

The zombie sprang, and Langston hit him with a flurry of punches to the chest. The zombie brought its fist around and smashed it into the side of Langston's head. Langston stumbled, and the zombie capitalized with an uppercut to the stomach. Langston grunted and bent at the waist. The zombie circled one arm around the boy's neck and threw himself back in a perfect DDT. Langston's face hit the asphalt and stars burst across his vision; the zombie clambered onto his back, put him in a one-armed chokehold, and pressed his knee between Langston's shoulder blades, trapping him. "Tap out," the zombie said.

"Never!" Langston cried.

The zombie tightened his grip, cutting off Langston's air supply. "Say uncle."

"Fuck you!"

The edges of Langston's consciousness turned soft and gray, and his lungs throbbed for air. Panic began to set in and hysteria threatened to overwhelm him.

Before losing control, he aligned his chakras (or something), and asked himself the one guiding question that had informed his life since seventh grade.

What would Bruce do?

Easy.

Bruce would *win.*

Gritting his teeth and calling upon reserves of strength he didn't even know he had, Langston bucked like an untamed bronco, and the zombie's hold loosened. Its arm brushed Langston's lips, and seeing his chance, he bit down as hard as he could, teeth rending, jaw locking; cold, dead skin flecking his tongue like the world's yuckiest spice. The zombie howled in pain, and Langston bucked again, this time knocking him off.

He jumped to his feet, and the zombie rolled back and forth like a turtle on its shell, holding its wounded forearm and hissing like Peter Griffin with a skinned knee. "God," it moaned, "that really *does* hurt."

Langston lifted his foot, and the zombie's eyes widened.

"You have been defeated," Langston said. Imagine the movements of his mouth not synching with what he says, just like a dubbed Bruce Lee movie.

The zombie held up its hands in a mollifying gesture. "Wait, please, don't. Before you kill me...let me pray."

Langston stopped. As a god-fearing type himself, he understood and respected the zombie's desire to get right with the big guy. "Fine. Pray."

The zombie balled his fists to his mouth and closed his eyes. "Dear Heavenly Father, I beg of you: Give this son of a bitch dick rot for me."

Snarling, Langston brought his foot down on the zombie's face, breaking its head like an overripe pumpkin.

He yanked away and turned just as another ghoul came up the street, this one tall and broad with cornrows. Clad in jeans and a white T-shirt caked in dirt, it looked left and right like a stranger in a strange land.

More foes.

Langston strode toward him.

Wilko saw him and stopped, one corner of his mouth lifting in a sneer of distaste. Langston stopped in front of him, held up his fists, and weaved his head from side to side. Energy flowed through him and for the first time he could remember, he felt truly at peace with the world.

All it took was killing a bunch of people.

Well..."people."

"What the fuck is you doin'?" Wilko asked.

Langston scuttled closer, ready to strike.

"You best get yo' lil' headband-wearin' ass out my grill, nigga. I ain't tryna fuck wit'cho. Go on."

He tried to walk around, but Langston blocked his path. "I've come to destroy you."

Wilko's brow shot up. "Oh, you ain't gonna do shit to *me*, nigga."

Langston held a hand out, palm up, and curled his fingers in a defiant come-hither.

"'Ight," Wilko said. He took a diamond stud out of his ear and shoved it into the hands of a passing zombie. "Hold my shit." He rolled his neck, squared his shoulders, and cracked his knuckles with a flourish. "You really tryna get'cho feelin's hurt?"

Langston's only response was to bounce from one foot to the other.

"Make yo' move, homie," Wilko said.

Tensing, Langston did...and the white rapper instantly grabbed him by the throat and dragged him off his feet, just like he did with Tim. Must be part of his MO. "What's good, homie?" he yelled obnoxiously. "What's good?"

For the second time that night, Langston couldn't breathe. He thrashed, kicked, and pummeled Wilko's face with blows, but none of those shots had any effect on the gargantuan. Langston's brain spasmed in terror and his lungs squeezed in a vise. His eyes bugged from their sockets and the warm, tingling mist of death settled over him. He frantically clawed at the backs of Wilko's hands, but to no avail. He swung his legs up, planted his feet into Wilko's stomach, and tried to pull back, but that didn't work. It wasn't looking good, folks.

"You gon' die tonight, nigga. You gon' get'cho ass back up and walk around just like me. You gon' feel yo'self rot, nigga. You gon' be cold as fuck too, nigga."

Langston's life flashed before his eyes...and the final image was Bruce Lee looking disappointed. *You let me down, Langston.*

Sensi, no!

Crying out, he hit Wilko dead in the nose. It shattered under his fist and the SoundCloud-wannabe's hands flew open. Langston dropped to his knees, then got back to his feet just in time for Wilko to grab him again. This time, instead of choking him, Wilko spun him around and let go.

For a terrible second, Langston screamed through the night...then he landed hard on the grass, the air whooshing from his lungs. He lay there, stunned, then rolled onto his stomach and got his hands and knees under him.

"You motherfucka!" Wilko roared.

He snatched Langston up by his shaggy blonde hair and pulled him to his feet. Langston twisted around and hit him in the mid-section with a devastating punch. Wilko staggered, then came forward like a freight train. Langston tried to jump out of the way, but he wasn't fast enough; Wilko tackled him into something stone, rough, and abrasive. Langston's flesh tore, blood tickled. Everything hurt: His muscles, his legs, and his arms.

Wilko hit him once, twice, three times, left, right, left, right. He closed his hand around Langston's throat, reared back, and lifted his fist for one last punch, this one lethal. Langston closed his eyes...

...but the hit never came.

He creaked one eye open, and Wilko stared up at something looming over them. Langston followed his gaze.

The statue.

They were at its base; Langston bent back over the pedestal. The bronze figure towered above their heads, revealed by a spotlight pointed just so, that way people could bask in Wilko's greatness even after sundown. "*What?*" Wilko drew in amazement. He let Langston go and fisted his hand to his mouth. "Yo, they got a *statue* of me?"

Langston rolled to one side, fell to his knees in a heap, and fought to catch his breath. He was bloodied, dazed, and missing a tooth or two...but he was alive.

"Yo, look at this," Wilko beamed. "They even got me in my Phats, nigga. Word?" He walked slowly around the statue, craning his neck to take in every detail. Langston staggered to his feet, woozy, and swayed like a tree in a hurricane (can we nuke it?). Wilko climbed up onto the platform and studied his bronze counterpart like Narcissus at the reflecting pool. Langston lingered for a moment...then said screw it and stumbled away. He'd go pick on someone his own size.

Alone, Wilko pulled out his phone. "I'mma put this shit on Instagram," he said as he opened his camera.

Three minutes later, Wilko the White Rapper's 800,000 followers were shocked when the dead man's account updated for the first time in three years with a photo: A face, decaying and gray but recognizable as Wilko, mugging next to his statue.

THEY LOVE ME, the caption read.

Once all the doors and windows were boarded up, Dad, Tim, and Mark sank onto the couch next to Mom and Jess. I paced around the living room with my phone in my hand. I called the state police, the National Guard, and even the Department of Defense. The latter put me on hold. Uh, hello, zombies wait for no man.

Outside, the dead attacked the doors and windows. The table covering the front window trembled, and the entertainment system shook in place. The barricades - a haphazardly-slapped-together pile of wood scraps, interior doors, the coffee table, credenza, and other things - wouldn't hold for long; soon, they'd give way and the zombies would get in.

"Alright," Dad said, "how exactly did this happen? You read a book?"

Still pacing, I told him how I found Ellie Rimbugh's book at the library, what I learned about it, and then finally, about reading it as a joke. He listened intently, nodded here and there, and exhaled deeply when I was finished. The pounding filled the house, an apocalyptic din that made the walls seem closer, the air hotter. Jess hugged herself and Mom chewed her nails (her nails, not Jess's).

"Where is the book?" Dad asked. "Maybe there's a spell that'll send them back."

"I left it at the cemetery."

Dad groaned.

"I'm sorry! I didn't know this was going to happen!"

He sighed. "It's not your fault I wouldn't have believed that shit either."

The window flanking the door broke with a tinkle and the door nailed over it vibrated under the zombies' assault. "We can't stay here." Dad got to his feet and grabbed the AR-15 then jammed a new magazine into the stock.

"What are we going to do?" Mom asked incredulously. "Those things are everywhere. They'll tear us apart the moment we set foot outside."

"The car's in the driveway," Dad said. "Twenty feet away. If we can get to it, we can get out of here. And getting there shouldn't be too hard. Those things talk tough but they're a bunch of pussies."

"How?" Mom demanded. "You saw how many are out there. Even with the guns, we'll be kibble in seconds."

Jess whimpered, and Mark slipped his arm around her shoulders.

"And where will we go?" Mom continued.

Dad pulled back the gun's lever and chambered a round. *Clack.* "To get that book."

Terror pooled in Jess's eyes and she rocked faster, shaking her head no.

"I say we just leave town," Mark said. "Problem solved."

"And let those undead assholes eat everyone we love?" Dad asked. "Your parents? Your friends?"

Mark didn't have a rebuttal for *that*.

Shoving the .357 into his waistband, Dad slung the rifle over his shoulder, reached into the box, and brought out an Uzi.

Jesus, Dad, now you're scaring me. I knew you liked guns, but holy arsenal. What else you got in there, a bazooka?

Actually, that might come in handy right about now.

Mom stood up and raked her hands through her hair. It started the evening in a professional bun, but over the course of the past half hour, strands had worked free and hung limply in her face, lending her a frazzled appearance. "Before we do anything or go anywhere, we have to worry about getting to the car." She gestured to the door. "How are we going to do that with a million zombies trying to get in?"

"Maybe a distraction," Tim spoke up, and everyone looked at him. "One of us runs, leads them away, then the others swing by and pick them up."

Dad considered the plan, then rejected it. "Nah, that won't work. Those things will be on top of the car like *that*. It's too dangerous."

Darn. That was actually a good idea, too. I stared down at my gun and wracked my brain. Alright, Dad said you got us into this mess and he wasn't just whistling Dixie. You did.

But Alex -

No buts, Alex. Maybe that book exerts some kind of power, but this wouldn't be happening if you didn't read it in the middle of the cemetery like a doofus. It's up to you to save the day. Your parents, your Tim, and your Jess are on the line here.

And Mark too. Can't forget him.

Think...think...

Then it hit me like a pie to the face. "I know what we can do!"

Mom, Dad, Mark, and Tim all turned to me. Jess kept on rocking and breathing through her nose, trying to stave off a total emotional breakdown...or epic gas.

"What?" Dad asked.

"I saw it in *The Walking Dead* one time."

"What?"

I held up my pointer finger. "First, we get some bed sheets and put them on. Second, we get a zombie. Third, we cut the zombie open, smear its guts on the bed sheets, and then walk outside. The zombies will think we're one of them and ignore us. Fourth, we get in the car, put on our seatbelts, and cruise out of here in *style.*"

Mom and Dad looked at each other, and a thought passed between them. "That's the stupidest idea I've ever heard," Dad said.

"Really, Alex, why not just slather ourselves in BBQ sauce while we're at it?" Mom asked.

Eyeroll. Everyone's a critic. "Do you have a better idea?"

The clatter of the dead trying to break their way in reached a fever pitch. The entertainment center shifted, and the door opened just wide enough for a half dozen arms to get through. Dad and Tim hurried over and threw themselves against the blockade. "We're gonna have to fight our way out," Dad called.

What? No.

"That's insane!" Mom yelled. "We can't do that!"

Leaving Jess's side, Mark picked the hammer up from the coffee table, went to the door, and smashed the claw end into one of the hands. He hit another, and another, and one by one, they slithered away until Dad and Tim were able to get the door closed.

"What's the situation out back?" Dad asked.

I rushed into the kitchen ahead of Mom, splayed my hands on the counter and leaned over to see out the window above the sink - it was too high for zombies to reach, so Dad left it uncovered. In the backyard, a couple zombies stumbled around like guys on a jobsite with nothing to do. One trampled Mom's rose garden, and she gasped. "Hey! Get out of my roses!"

The zombie looked up toward the window. "Yeah, I'm talking to you, no nose."

Back in the living room, Dad, Tim, and Mark had shoved one end of the couch against the entertainment center. It was a fold-out, and heavy as a mofo. Jess was perched on the edge, no longer rocking but still traumatized; she stared into space and rubbed her hands along her arms as if for warmth, her breathing so shallow as to be nearly nonexistent.

"There're a couple," I said, "but not many."

Dad pursed his lips in thought. "Alright, we'll go out the back and around the side. If we stay low and quiet, we can get to the car."

"I-I can't go out there." Jess stuttered. "M-my ankle. I-I twisted it."

"Goddamn it," Dad sighed. He glanced up the stairs, then to the door; the entertainment center trembled, and beyond it, the door cracked under the barrage. "Alright," he said, "you stay here. Maria and Mark, you stay with her."

My heart sank. Mom and Jess...staying behind? "W-We can't leave them."

"We don't have any other choice." They'll be safe in the attic."

Mark and Dad helped Jess up the stairs and Tim took up position in front of the entertainment center with a shotgun; he looked so much like Elmer Fudd hunting wabbits that I would have laughed under other circumstances.

In the second floor hall, Dad pulled the cord and the accordion stairs folded down. Mom went up first with a flashlight, made sure it was safe, and called down for Jess to come up.

"Can you make it on your own?" Dad asked.

She nodded, and favoring her bad foot, scurried up the ladder. Dad turned to Mark, un-shouldered his AR-15 and handed it to him. "This is an AR-15; the clip holds 99 gas-tipped bullets and the chamber fires at a rate of twenty rounds per millisecond. It doesn't matter where you hit your target, it will instantly die. One shot has enough terminal velocity to cut through ten feet of concrete. All you have to do is hold the trigger down and rain hell at whatever you want to die."

Mark took the gun with a puzzled frown. "I don't know much about guns, Mr. Warner, but I think you got a few things wrong there."

Clapping Mark on the arm, Dad said, "Not if you ask a liberal."

Before we went back downstairs, I climbed up the ladder to say goodbye to Mom and Jess. Mark sat to one side with the rifle propped between his knees, and Jess rubbed her ankle with a grimace. "Be careful," Mom said and hugged me fiercely.

"I will."

I turned to Jess. I'm not a very good writer even though I might like to think otherwise, and there's no way I could even begin to describe what my sister means to me. I know I have a reputation for playing and being silly, but...a long time ago, a little girl came to live with me and my parents, a little girl who had just lost her own mother and father. She didn't fully understand death, I think, but she knew her mommy and daddy weren't there, and she was alone with strange people she barely knew. She was like...I don't know, a sad little lamb or something. Mom told me once as she tucked me into bed that I had to look out for my little cousin because she needed me, and I vowed that I would.

Over the years, Jess and I have had some pretty wacky adventures. We've fought, bickered, played, and no matter what, we've always been there for each other.

Emotion welled in my throat, and I blinked away the tears forming in my eyes. 'I'm sorry," I said earnestly. "I should have listened to you about that book. You were right and I was wrong. Like usual." I took her hand. "This is all my fault. I was dumb and selfish and if we just stayed home and watched TV together, we wouldn't be in this mess."

She drew a deep breath and let it out through her nose. "I'm not worried about that," she said. "If you want to show me you're sorry...do me a favor."

"What?"

"Be careful out there."

We hugged, then feeling a mixture of shame, guilt, and fear, I left her and Mom in the care of Mark. "You better not screw this up, buddy," I told him.

"I won't," he promised.

Dad gave Mom and Jess both a kiss, and Mom hugged him. "No stupid shit," she said. "And watch out for our little girl."

"I will." He stroked her cheek. "Then, when this is over, I'm grounding her."

"Me too," Mom said.

Ugh.

Downstairs, the entertainment center had begun to split and fissure and the couch to move. Seven arms, now eight, reached through the gap between the window sill and the coffee table. Hands gripped the edge and worked the table back and forth trying to free it.

"Stop," Tim begged.

"'Stop,'" a zombie mocked.

"We're gonna eat'cha," another taunted.

"I call his nuts."

Dad grabbed the Uzi from the couch, slipped the strap over his shoulder, and handed Tim a Glock. "Here's the plan."

Five minutes later, we huddled around the back door, Dad with one hand on the knob and the Uzi in the other. "On the count of three, Alex, stay right behind me. Tim, bring up the rear. If you have to, let them eat you while we get away."

"Dad!"

"I said only if he has to."

He curled his finger around the trigger. "One…"

I checked my gun to make sure the safety was off. Heh. Bet'cha thought I was gonna forget.

"Two…"

Tim pumped the shotgun. *Chu-chu.*

"…three!"

Dad pulled the door open and went out low and fast. I followed, and Tim came behind, pulling it closed and locking it behind him. The three zombies in the backyard stumbled toward us. Dad ran at the closest and threw a punch that drove it back into the others. He darted around the side of the house and I stayed hot on his heels.

A narrow strip of yard runs between our house and the wood stockade fence trimming Mr. Krause's property. The tree branches overhead blotted out the moon, and for a second, the darkness was total.

Dad stopped at the corner and I came to a halt next to him. He leaned over to see around it, then glanced at me and Tim. "Stay down and be quiet."

I nodded, too scared to speak. From here, the pounding wasn't as loud as it was inside, but the moaning was clear and chilling.

Not waiting, Dad hunched over and darted out from cover. I took his place and peeked around the corner post: The car sat to my right at the head of the driveway. Dad ducked behind the front end and crept to the passenger door. The zombies from the backyard were closing in, and Tim brought the butt of the shotgun up and rammed it into one's face, knocking it down. The other reached for him, and pushing it away, he kicked it in the stomach, folding it over, then crashed his knee into its face. The cacophony of moans and hissing covered the sounds of the scuffle

Dad eased the door open and slipped in. Taking a deep breath, I crouched and hurried to the car. I climbed into the passenger seat and Tim got in the back. Behind the wheel, Dad looked pleased with himself. "That went a lot easier than I thought it would." He patted his hip pocket...then sagged.

"What?" I asked.

"I forgot to get the keys from your mom."

My heart sank. "Really???"

"No worries," he said. "I can hotwire it."

In the back, Tim gulped. "You better hurry."

All of the zombies that had been trying to get in the front - four dozen at least - were shambling toward the car. "Fuck," Dad whispered.

He ripped off the plastic paneling under the wheel and dug frantically in the mess of wires. The zombies reached the car and closed around it in a black, spreading tide, blocking the light, slapping the windshield, and rocking the frame. One tried to pull my door open, and another smooshed its face against Dad's window, its teeth chattering spasmodically (give me your braaaaain, Mr. Warner). The car pitched side-to-side like a boat in stormy swells, and I held on for dear life.

"Hurry!" I screamed.

Dad cussed under his breath and pulled two wires out to see them better. "I think it's these two."

My window exploded, and cold fingers threaded through my hair. I let out a high pitched squeal, and tried to pull away. "I got her!" the zombie cried triumphantly. He yanked my head to the side, and a shard of glass gashed my cheek, sending stinging pain into my head. Tim leaned over and jabbed the barrel of the shotgun against the zombie's face, pushing him back.

"Aha," Dad said. He crossed two wires and the engine roared into life. He threw it in reverse and hit the gas; we rocketed backwards, and the hand released my hair as the zombie attached to it lost its footing and went down.

Dad spun the wheel, and we angled sharply to the left, the tires leaving the driveway and tearing up the grass. We hit the mailbox and the trash cans, then Dad slammed on the brakes, throwing me against the dash. Ow. I really need to start wearing my seatbelt.

The zombies ran after us, and Dad put the car in drive; he hit the gas, and I flopped back against my seat like a ragdoll. A few ghouls coming down the middle of the street jumped out of our way, and Dad swerved to miss a few bent over eating something. For a heart-stopping second, I thought it was a wayward trick-or-treater, but it was only roadkill.

Whew.

In the rearview mirror, the zombies dwindled until they were gone, and I let out a breath I didn't know I was holding. I hoped they all followed us and none tried getting into the house. Mark, Mom, and Jess should be okay where they were, but these weren't your garden variety Romero zombies; these were black magic psychopaths.

Dad took a sharp corner, and the wheels screeched on the pavement. "When we get there, find this damn book and make these assholes go back where they came from, alright?"

"I will."

If I can find it, I added to myself. Remember, I had no clue what I was even looking for. I started reading the last spell totally at random. Those words could have literally meant anything - they could have made puppies, kittens, and free healthcare rain from the sky and I would have been none the wiser. Funny thing: I don't even know what I said back at Westvale. I remember the words *terra* and *ad hoc.* What did those even mean?

On Main Street, a zombie ambled hurriedly down the sidewalk like it was fleeing something, casting a worried glance over its shoulder. Dad turned, but right before he did, I swore I saw a shirtless Langston stalking after it.

We reached the cemetery five minutes later. A lot of body parts were strewn across the ground, a macabre confusion of arms, legs, and other human detritus that you'd need a pathologist and full-scale dental records to identify. With so many decades-old corpses walking around, it stood to reason some of them would kind of...shed.

Shiver.

Dad parked behind Tim's car and got out, leaving the engine running. The gate stood open, and I couldn't help feeling like it wasn't an entrance at all, but a big, hungry mouth. Tim jerked an overwrought look around and Dad held the Uzi tight to his chest. A cold wind rustled the trees, but otherwise, nothing moved; the world was silent, dead, the plague demon moved on to the other side of town. How many people in the houses between here and home had been killed by zombies? How many men and women torn apart and eaten? How many terrified children ripped from their parents' arms and murdered all because of me?

Hot tears flooded my eyes and I cut that thought off. If I started thinking about stuff like that, I'd go to pieces.

"Keep together," Dad said. His voice was low and bloodless, and the moonlight glinted in his big, unblinking eyes. For the first time all night, he looked afraid. I swallowed and turned away. I tease him a lot, but my dad's the strongest and bravest dude I know; knowing *he* was scared made *me* even more scared than I already was.

He pointed the Uzi out in front of him and went through the gate, gravel crunching under his feet. Holes dotted the ground, marking the spots where the earth spat up a corpse; the wind knocked barren tree branches forlornly together. Tim swept the cemetery with the shotgun, and jumped when an owl hooted. Aw, poor baby. I patted him on the butt and he looked at me strangely.

"You're hot when you're armed."

I expected a blush and a giggle. Instead, I got a glare and a, "This is not the time for that, Alex."

Well then.

See if I ever compliment *you* again.

"Where are we going?" Dad asked.

We stopped and I scanned the cemetery. Tombstones huddled in the darkness and a skim of wind-driven leaves whispered along the overgrown grass. Something moved and I tensed;

seconds later, a skunk waddled out from behind a headstone shaped like a cross and disappeared into a gaping hole.

It never occurred to me, but the cemetery is really the safest place during a zombie apocalypse. All the dead people have already gotten up and gone forth in search of blood, leaving it empty. Heh. They can take over our world, but we'll just take over theirs.

Now where were we? In the night, everything had a dull sameness. I *thought* we were farther along the gravel road, but couldn't be sure. "This way," I said.

After a couple minutes of walking, we came to a wide, grassy area. This looked like the place. I ran my gaze over the ground, and when I saw the book, my heart jolted. "There!"

I brushed past Tim, bent, and picked it up. The cover – totally human skin, why was I in denial – throbbed in my hands, and the face seemed bigger than before. Dad leaned in over my shoulder, then shuddered. "That thing's creepy. You really had that thing sitting around the house for days?"

"She carried it around, too," Tim said. "Like a little girl with a teddy bear."

"I blame her mother."

"Nah, she's messed up on her own."

Flashing, I rammed my elbow into Tim's ribs, and he let out a breathless *oof.* "I'm not messed up."

Am I?

Reckoning that was a question for another day, I went to open the book, but a high, grating laugh stopped me.

Uh, what was that?

"Back again, I see."

The book.

It was talking.

Its mouth curved up in a wicked smile, and I blinked my eyes like a cartoon character. I'd seen a lot in the past couple hours...but this? Now *this* was pushing it.

"Holy shit," Tim breathed.

The book laughed again, its mouth making funny and - I felt - mocking shapes. "I'm surprised you made it. Not many people can withstand an army of the dead."

"Y-Yeah, w-we made it," I said. What's next, aliens? "Now, uh, how do we stop this?"

The owl hooted again, and the boughs of the trees rattled in the wind. "I'm not telling *you*," the book said, as though explaining something simple and obvious to a particularly stupid child. "This is the most fun I've had in centuries; do you really think I'm going to spoil it for myself?"

"Oh, come on," I said. "Please?"

The book made a show of mulling over my plea. "Nope, uh-uh."

I sighed. "Look, I know you've been locked up for a long time, and I'm sorry for that, but I did something really stupid tonight and put everyone I love in danger: My mom and my sister, my boyfriend, my dad...everyone in town. This is all my fault. I'm selfish, careless, and probably ADHD or something. I've hurt a lot of people and...and, I just want to make things okay. Please, *please* help me."

The book sighed, my appeal to its heart having succeeded. "Alright fine, you have swayed me. I will tell you how to send the dead back to their graves, but you *must* do exactly as I say. Understood?"

"Yes."

"First, set me down."

I carefully set the book in a soft tuft of grass and stood up straight. "All of you, get in a line."

Dad and Tim stood on either side of me. "Now...spin in a circle."

We all spun in stiff circles.

"Stop."

We stopped.

"Slap yourselves in the face."

I hesitated...then whacked myself with my open palm. Dad and Tim did likewise.

"Now...do *I'm A Little Tea Pot.*"

Uhh...okay? I put my hand on my hip and held my opposite arm out, palm up. Tim and Dad copied, and in unison, we sang. "I'm a little tea pot, short and stout. Here is my handle, here is my spout; when I get all steamed up, hear me shout. Tip me over and pour me out."

"Did that work?" I asked hopefully. "Are they going back to their graves?"

"No," the book shrieked with laughter. "I lied. And you three morons fell for it. Ahahahahahaha."

Growling, Dad grabbed the book and held it to his face. "Look asshole, I'm done playing games. Tell me how to get rid of these zombies or I'll blast you back to hell."

The book laughed. "Don't threaten *me* with a good time."

A long, low moan drifted through the cemetery, and my spirit withered. A group of zombies appeared at the gate; one poked his head in, saw us, and pointed. "There they are!"

"Shit," Dad hissed. He threw the book down and held the Uzi at his hip. Tim planted the butt of the shotgun in his shoulder and aimed; his hands trembled and his nostrils flared with ragged inhalations. "Alex," Dad said over his shoulder, "find that spell *now*."

Right.

I picked the book up and brushed my hair out of my face. "You better hurry," it said, "or all of the people you so *love* will be torn apart." It cackled, and my eyes narrowed. Making a fist with my hand, I flashed it up, then down, hitting its stupid, ugly face. Its satisfying cry of pain was sweet music to my ears, and I would have done it again, but Dad and Tim opened fire, startling me. Zombies streamed through the gate, rank after rank, ten across and twenty back. The first row absorbed the bullets, some falling, others merely staggering.

I opened the book and quickly went through the pages, ripping some of them in my haste. "Ahhh," the book yowled. "Be careful!"

Where is it? Where is it? Whereisitwhereisitwhereisitwhereisit? The shotgun roared, and Tim racked it, the empty casing flying from the chamber. Dad pulled the trigger, and fire leapt from the Uzi's barrel. *Tat-tat-tat-tat.* Zombies jerked, spun, and fell, but the seething mass continued its slow and inexorable march, treading them underfoot. Tim took aim at a woman in a burial dress, and her head exploded in a burst of broken skull and moldy brain matter. Dad raked fire low, and a couple zombies dropped. "My leg!" one screamed. "Oh, my leg!"

"Alex!" Dad shouted.

Right - off track: I really *am* ADHD. Where is it? Where is it? God, where is it? And what is it? I squinted to read by moonlight, didn't see anything that jumped out at me, and turned the page, ripping it. "Ouch!" My heart slammed, my stomach rolled, my entire body trembled, and pressure wound around my neck. The moaning was closer, closer, ever closer, and the gunfire slackened as Dad stopped to reload.

At the very end of the book, I came to a page written in Spanish. I glanced over the text, and my stomach sucked into my throat. I could read a little of Mom's native tongue, thanks to her stubborn insistence that I learn all things Mexican. I picked out *dead, back, ground,* and *stop.*

"I found it!" I exclaimed.

"Hurry!" Dad yelled. "They're getting closer."

The vanguard was twenty feet and closing, arms up, teeth gnashing, moans, hisses, and other hellish sounds rising from decaying vocal cords. A gust of wind flipped my hair in my face again, and I tucked it behind my ear.

Alright Alex, you read Latin earlier. After that, Spanish is a walk in the park.

Still, I felt like a little girl standing before a big, scary monster: Weak, powerless, afraid.

Swallowing my fear, I started to read...haltingly.

"M-Muertos, r-regresen a sus tumbas. Vuelve a dormir. D-Deja de hacer lo que estás haciendo y vuelve al suelo."

"Roll your Rs!" Dad commanded over his shoulder.

"I'm trying!"

The dead were ten feet from our position and closing in. Tim aimed dead center and fired, cutting three of them down.

"Gente muerta, váyanse, detengan esto ahora y dejen en paz a los vivos. Has vivido, ahora vuelve a la tierra."

The words felt like mush in my mouth and sounded like gibberish in my ears, but it was working: A stiff wind sprang up, and the trees whipped back and forth. Massive white clouds rolled across the sky like celestial mountains and lightning crackled in their depths. Energy went through me, just like before, and power. My hair writhed around my head, and I swear to God, I'm pretty sure I levitated six inches off the ground on a tide of magic. In that moment, understanding dawned on me, and I could see - all too clearly - why witches consort with Satan; like drugs, Satan makes you high...but in the end, he always brings you down low.

"¡Ir! Ve y nunca vuelvas!"

A whip-crack of thunder split the night like a Godly pronouncement, and the zombies stopped bare inches from Dad and Tim, who hugged each other and whimpered like babies.

For a moment, nothing happened, then, one-by-one, the dead began drifting away, some of them mumbling under their breath and others yawning as though suddenly exhausted. I watched, stunned as they returned to their graves, and a big, shit-eating grin spread across my face.

It was over.

I did it.

I actually *freaking* did it.

"Noooo," the book lamented. "My good time."

I snapped the cover closed, and tears leaked from the face's eyes.

Being petty, I stuck out my tongue.

Close to me, a zombie wiggled into a hole, only for another to shuffle up. "That's *my* grave, buddy, yours is over there." He hooked a thumb over his shoulder.

"Whoops, my mistake."

Someone bumped into me, and I turned.

My spirits crashed.

A zombie with a half skeletal face glared at me. I held the book up like a shield and cringed, but the ghoul made no move to attack. "Don't wake me up again," he said.

"Yeah," another called from its grave, "leave us alone."

"Don't you know children shouldn't play with dead things?" the first one demanded.

I opened my mouth, but shaking its head, it waved me off and shambled away.

Well...I know *now*.

A hand fell on my shoulder, and I whipped around, but it was just Dad. His face was dirty and covered in sweat. "Where'd the dirt come from?"

"One of those assholes threw a dirt ball at me."

"Pegged him in the nose too!" a zombie called and the legion of the dead erupted in laughter.

He looked like he wanted to say something, then pulled me into a hug. "I'm glad you're okay." His voice welled with emotion and I swallowed a cold lump. "I was...a *little* scared." It was clear from his tone that he was actually *a lot* scared.

"I was too," I said, "but only a little."

Tim leaned on the shotgun like a cane, and when a dead woman in a pink dress passed close, he cringed. She stopped, flicked her eyes up and down his body, and gave a suggestive wink.

I walked over, but he was too busy staring after his new girlfriend to notice. "You okay?" He jumped.

"Yeah." He looked nervously over his shoulder as a deader waddled past. "I'm fine." He showed a wan smile that was cute despite its pallor.

I rubbed the back of my neck. "I-I'm sorry about this. You know, raising the dead and putting us all in mortal danger. I promise it won't happen again."

Tim grinned. "Well, this was certainly a Halloween I'll never forget."

We hugged, and after all we'd been through that night, being in his arms made everything alright.

"Come on," Dad called from near the gate. "I wanna get home and check on your mom and Jess."

Hand-in-hand, Tim and I left that place of the dead. At the gate, Dad waited by the car, warily watching zombies file past like bone-weary convicts returning to their cells after a long day of breaking rocks. Wilko the White Rapper stopped next to Tim's car and squinted down at his iPhone.

"Yes, nigga," he said as his thumbs flew across the screen, "it's really me." He shook his head and shoved the phone into his pocket. "These niggas trippin'. Act like they ain't ever seen a dead man be'fo."

On the car ride home, we passed a dozen zombies heading in the direction of the cemetery. None of them made any move to attack us; none of them even looked at us. Gray State Police cruisers were scattered around downtown and troopers in riot gear stood idle, revelers too late to the party and not realizing it. A block from home, the headlights washed over a figure sitting despondently on the curb, its face resting in its upturned palms. It was tall, kinda pudgy, and shirtless.

Langston.

"Slow down," I told Dad.

We stopped next to him and I rolled down my window. "Yo, Langston."

He looked up, and the puppy dog sadness in his eyes caught me off guard. "I was having fun," he muttered.

Oh. I wasn't. "I'm sorry." I lied, "You want a ride?"

He took a big, watery breath. "No, I wanna sulk."

"...Okay. Uh...have a good night."

I like Langston...a lot, he's a cool guy...but he's also a giant weirdo.

At home, we pulled into the driveway and got out. The night was silent save for the quiet cricket nocturne, a sound that once represented the

122

epitome of boring to me but now represented peace.

The back door was closed, as Tim had left it, and the kitchen and living room brightly lit but deserted, making it somehow more eerie than the dark, cold cemetery. Upstairs, Dad pulled the cord and the folding door dropped. "It's us," he called.

After a moment, Mom's head appeared. "Is it over?"

Dad nodded. "Yeah. We did it."

"Thank God," she sighed.

She, Mark, and Jess climbed down the steps, and at the bottom, she hugged me. "I'm proud of you," she said and held me at arm's length.

"For waking the dead?" I asked wryly.

"For cleaning up the mess you made. That shows responsibility."

A flush of pride came over me.

"You're still grounded, through."

I opened my mouth to protest, but...you know what? Considering all that happened, that wasn't so bad. My family was safe, the world was saved, and I later learned not a single person died in Pickett's Meade that night. A grounding was a small, small price to pay for that.

CHAPTER SIX

"Please...please don't put me back. I'll do *anything*. I promise. I can make your wildest dreams come true. I can make you rich and powerful."

I knelt in the attic on the bright morning of November 1, a warm shaft of sunlight falling across my lap. In Mexico, it was the Day of the Dead, a holiday where people celebrate those who are now gone. If I had any grace and timing at all, I would have waited until today to wake the dead – more fitting that way. I held the book in my hands and scrunched my lips thoughtfully back and forth. Next to me, Jess flicked her eyes uneasily between us.

"Don't listen to it," she said anxiously.

"*Do* listen to me," the book begged. "I'll do anything; just don't lock me up again. *Please*."

Untold riches, huh? Fame to my heart's desire? Anything I want?

I looked at Jess, then at the book. "Sorry, I already have everything I want."

Leaning over, I set it in a metal lockbox.

"Wait! No, wait!"

I closed the lid, locked it, and put the key in my pocket. I picked the box up, got to my feet, and carried it to the farthest, darkest corner, where I set it down. I put a tattered cardboard box on top of it, and pushed a trunk against it, completely boxing it in. The book's sobbing was muffled, but still audible.

Dusting my hands, I turned to Jess. "You thought I was actually going to listen to it, huh? Glad to see you think so highly of me."

"Alex...you literally caused an invasion of zombies last night."

I sighed and shook my head. "Jess, Jess, Jess...stuck in the past."

She rolled her eyes.

Reaching up, I pulled the light cord and plunged the attic into darkness. We climbed down and I closed the door. It thumped into place with grim finality, and I nudged Jess in the ribs. "Wanna watch a horror movie?"

"No."

I stuck out my bottom lip. "Pwese? I just wanna hang out with my sister."

She considered for a moment, a battle raging in her eyes, then let out a deep, burdened sigh. "Fine," she said, "but *not* about zombies."

"Deal."

With that, we went off to watch *The Texas Chain Saw Massacre.*

And everything was right in the world.

Joseph Rubas is, according to some, a mediocre author who wants to be Stephen King but can barely pull off Dean Koontz. To others, he's a genius. Read this book to find out which it is.

COMING SOON FROM NIGHTMARE PRESS:

Retro Horror
An anthology

The Cursed Diary of a Brooklyn Dog Walker
Michael Reyes

The Untaken
Bekki Pate

All Roads Lead
Jennifer Winters

Viva La Muerte
Quinn Hernandez

In Dormancy, They Sleep
D.G. Sutter

Todd Sullivan Presents: The Vampire Connoisseur
A vampire anthology

Slaughter at Seabridge
Cassidy Frost

The Passing
Joseph Rubas

Horrifica
Sheldon Woodbury